With these bags on my shoulders

Twenty-seven- year old, Amarylis Scott was a Southern Belle from Historic Georgetown, South Carolina. "Amarylis" meaning sparkling eyes, was the apple of Granny Estelle's eyes. Unlucky at finding and keeping a man, Amarylis stayed on the go. Juggling failed relationships were taking a toll on her. It was much easier for her to move from place to place and start over. Easy on the eye, Amarylis had a pretty face and a mean attitude. Most guys were afraid to speak to her or ask her about her day. If you did, she would growl and bite your head off. After every break-up, Amarylis just packed her worn duffle bags and swung them over her shoulders. She was tired of crying and eating boxes of chocolate. It had to be her or him. Whenever times got rough, Amarylis split without giving the guy a reasonable explanation as to why. Amarylis could easily be spotted strutting up the road with a switch in her hipsy blue jeans. She pretended not to have a care

Sparkle Riley

in the world while wobbling in her four-inch stilettos. She would just roll her crimpy bangs up in wet pink setting lotion and then snap it in pink spongy rollers. There was no shame in her game. Amarylis was not worrying about impressing nobody! She would simply put her floral scarf around her head and called it a day. She was the epic of Southern Hospitality's finest with a bad chip on her shoulder, thanks to her Granny and Birdie. In her life, there was no such things as reasons, excuses or explanations. You got to leave before you get left. Nobody had ever given her a reason about anything, so she never expected one. It was easier that way for her if that makes sense. Everybody in her life did exactly that. It tore her down not knowing the unknown. Being the only child in a single parent home was anything but peaches and cream for her. Her dad, nameless and unimaginable left before she was born with no explanation as to why. Her Mama, Birdie Scott ran off with some man and that was that. Her own mama looked right in her face and said nothing to her about it. Where was she going? Why couldn't she go to? Why was that strange man taking her mommy away? Amarylis was just eight, when Birdie dropped her off on her Granny's front porch. A chubby little thang with two nappy

Sparkle Riley

pigtails and wearing a swirly flowered lavender sundress. It was all

lacey and girly. The sweltering heat made all the Murray's grease

drip down her round face. Little Amaryllis just stood there twirling

her pigtails with her fingers. The bags on her shoulders felt so light

in weight. Her mama was in such a hurry to leave that day. The

man in the car kept blowing his horn for mama to come out. Birdie

did not have time to pack her toys or nothing. Her favorite Baby

Dollie and Teddy Bear that she liked so much were left behind.

Birdie never gave her a heads up or nothing. Her mama gave her

a few pairs of panties and some raggedy wrinkled clothes and that

was it. Birdie could have at least ironed her clothes. No goodbyes

or contact information, nothing. Amarylis could smell her musty

sneakers in one of her packed duffle bags. Why Birdie had to pack

them old nasty shoes, thought little Amarylis? Them things were

so worn that ants crawled through its holes and made a home in it.

All she had was a torn, bug ridden duffle bag on her back. Poor

Amarylis, had no clue as to why she was there? Was her Granny

Estelle expected her? The whole car ride there was silent. All you

could hear were the blue birds chirping and the wind blowing.

Even when they arrived at Granny's, Mama Birdie acted like she

Sparkle Riley

was invisible. So, she just stood there fiddling with the hem of her sundress. She looked down at her dirty gray slouch socks inside of her peeling flip flops. Granny Estelle never asked Birdie any questions. Granny grabbed her inside and never gave her any excuses or false hopes. Birdie was just gone. Granny took her in and that was that. That was ok with her because she did not have a choice in the matter either way. So, she just kept her mouth shut and never asked about her from that day on. In school, the kids did not like her at all! Was it because she was short and stocky and heavy handed? Was it her old-fashioned, pleated rainbow-colored skirts? Or was it her thrift store silk blouses that she wore every day? Letting Granny help her get ready for school played a big part in it too. Granny drowned her in old smelly Chantilly Perfume to be dainty and ladylike. Amaryllis would have preferred to wear bug spray than that stinky spray. At least the bug repellent would have kept the Fruit Flies and the Gnats away. That was the thing about old folks like Granny Estelle. They were so prissy and cheaply classy. You had to wash up in an old basin with Lilac soap and she hated that. The water would turn all murky and brown when the soap suds disappeared. Amarylis was a plain jane by the

Sparkle Riley

likes of who else, Granny. Amarylis kept her nappy hair pulled back in a snatch back with a pink flower on the side, pinned with wiry bobby pins. She had a little gap in her front teeth, that hardly anybody ever noticed. Amarylis was always quiet in school and kept to herself. There was never a reason to talk to the other kids at school. Who would want to be friends with her? The kids in her class did not even want to sit beside her! In her mind, nothing would have made a difference. The children just did not like her, plain and simple. No reason or clues were ever given, that she was aware of. It was like that all through school. After a while, that shit did not make a difference anyway. Her face was always real greasy from caked on Petroleum Jelly. As Granny would say, "you're too black to be ashy!" It was either that or she smelled like Moth balls and Ben-Gay Cream. If only she could go back and have tea parties with her again. Granny was the only person that she ever loved. With her cinnamon wrinkly colored stockings and floral housecoats. Amarylis had enough fig bars and butterscotch candies to last a lifetime. Prune juice and raisins sort of grew on her overtime, too. That was pretty much her childhood. An isolated loner with no friends. They acted like she was invisible in school.

5

Sparkle Riley

Amarylis never knew why? But when Granny hummed in her rocking chair, the outside world no longer mattered. The way that woman fanned her face while chewing snuff was priceless to her. Until at the age of seventeen, when she came home to find her Granny face down in the tub from an apparent suicide. Her Granny was the one person she thought would never just roll out on her like that. No suicide note, no words scribbled on a sticky pad, nada. For years that messed her head up and made her into the woman she is to today. A no cares, kind of screw you first mentality. Even after Granny died, she stayed in that big old country house. Granny's room was just off limits for the time being. Not properly processing and accepting her untimely death put her into a slump. Corn liquor was her salvage and her companion on those sultry summer nights. One day, drunk and volatile, she burst through Granny's room in a rage. She ripped and tore her room up looking for answers and explanations as to why she took her own life. Amarylis needed something, anything to explain why her Granny left her alone like that. But after graduation, she decided to sow her wild oats. Looking for valuables to pawn, she scurried Granny's room to finance her road

Sparkle Riley

trip. She desperately searched for anything of value. Slamming

open drawers. Breaking up jewelry boxes came up as a waste of

time. It was when she flipped her old squeaky bed over to reveal

popped springs. What she found changed her life. A clinic office

note that diagnosed Granny with Stage 2 Cancer. That coward

thought Amarylis, why would she do that? No reasonings of the

unknown, just kill yourself. Before knowing your treatment

options. It just did not make sense for her to just give up that.

Doctors have mistakenly misdiagnosed patients for ages. That

decision was up to God to decide at the end of the day. Cancer did

not have to be a death sentence for her. It is difficult not knowing

whether you are going to live or die from it. There was always a

possibility that Granny Estelle might could have beat it and out

lived her! That right there transformed her into the woman that she

is today, too.

At the precocious age of twenty, Amarylis fell in love with

the man of her dreams. Tall, sexy and caramel colored. The perfect

man. One who loved and adored her. Kyle Jacobs worshipped the

ground that she walked on. Kyle even got on one knee and

proposed and everything. Amarylis accepted and a fairytale

Sparkle Riley

wedding was planned. It was a June wedding at United Methodist Church over on Pine Road. A church overfilled with guests from all walks of life. A private orchestra distracted the guests from the seeing the pandemonium on her face. Heirlooms of Bridesmaids in sparkling diamond fused gowns. A choir ready to bless everyone with their beautiful voices. Hundreds of bouquets twirled around the pews. Sincere smiles and big church hats filled the atmosphere. All in attendance, except for her Groom. No unexplained emergencies, no texts, nothing. He left Amarylis Scott standing at the altar feeling embarrassed and stupid. Years after that, there was Steven, Corey, Winston and Ashtin. all rolled out and disappeared without a trace. No goodbye or see you later, nada. Everybody that she had ever loved just up and left her. They never took her feelings into account. That closed her heart at loving another man ever again. Amarylis ran away from love every chance she got. If a guy were too sweet and charming, she had run through his pockets like water. Once he was penniless and dry, she would leave them out of the blue. She would block them or simply change her phone number. If the sex was too good, her insecurities got the best of her. She assumed that she would always have to share her man

Sparkle Riley

with other women, so she cheated on them with a vengeance. It was much better and wiser to protect her heart and body by all costs. It helped her form acceptable unattachments to them more easily. It was personal and justifiable for her to just have sexual encounters with them and take all she could from them. Loving people was too painful and traumatic for her. Her scars bled and bruised and never fully healed!

Now, running from job to job was a new nasty habit for Amarylis. When it got to complicated or comfortable, she just up and quit. Her Supervisors acted like they cared about her to get what they wanted from her. Amarylis worked long hard hours for an extremely low pay rate. Her male bosses were even worse. Amarylis believed that had secretly wanted to take her to bed in order to get the salary she deserved. She did not give them a two-week notice or anything. It was a hardship and a blessing for her because she would rather quit than be fired for no explanation. She would rather be broke, without a cent to her name. At least she would have a piece of mind. She could live with being penniless and down to her last dollar rather than get fired. Now with a total of two thousand dollars and three bags on her shoulders, she was

Sparkle Riley

ready. She had always wanted to live in Baltimore City. Amarylis googled Baltimore Craig List for rooms to rent. She found some affordable places on the East side. With a Greyhound ticket and a flip phone in hand, it was time to board the bus. It was time for a new beginning, a change of scenery and a new life. Amarylis was ready for that 15- hour bus ride because it was worth it! It had to be because South Carolina was for the birds lol.

Sitting in the third row of the crowded Greyhound Amarylis was reading through the Baltimore Want Ads for a gig. If push came to shove, she could always strip. If not, a Sugar daddy would have to do. Something just got to give, thought Amarylis. "I can't get through life with just these bags on my shoulders" said Amarylis under her breath while rolling her eyes with an attitude.

Amarylis had a hard time concentrating on the newspaper in her hand. She had been dealt bad cards in her life for too long. It just was not fair to lose everything that you loved. All Amarylis ever wanted was to be loved back. She was always willing to give others more than what she got back. Amarylis wanted to be a good girlfriend, lover and companion but she was often taken advantage of. Kyle Jacobs left her standing at the Altar on their wedding day.

Sparkle Riley

She was supposed to be Mrs. Amarylis Jacobs. She worshipped the ground that he walked on too. She was the perfect fiancée and lover and he still left without a trace. Then there was Steven he conned her out of all her paychecks. She gave him every cent to help him buy a car. He said he loved her and wanted to spend the rest of his life with her and she believed him. Once he had enough to buy his dream car, Steven just vanished without a trace. Amarylis was living with a guy named Corey for months. He promised to take care of her. He told her to quit her job because he was the man of the house. Yes, he had naked pictures of ladies in his phone. Amarylis let a lot of things slide because she was dependent on him. When you are so in love, it is easy to ignore the red flags. His phone was always on vibrate around her. Corey would leave at 2am in the morning to go jogging. There was always lipstick on his collar or the scent of perfume on his jacket. It did not really bother her as much because Corey came home to her bed every night. It was not until the day that she heard loud banging on their apartment door, that reality had set in. Corey was not the man she thought she knew. The Sheriff and the landlord came to their apartment to forcibly evict her. Most of Corey's

Sparkle Riley

valuables were already gone. He hid the eviction notices from her for months. He never told her that he was behind in the rent. Her was eviction was to be carried out at that very moment. Amarylis watched in horror as her personal and intimate things were thrown out into the streets! The only pictures that she had of Birdie and Estelle were cracked and ripped. Corey could have given her a heads up or something. After the eviction, she never heard from him again. He changed his number and everything. But she bet he was still driving the car that she brought for him! I mean these guys were just coming at her left and right. Winston was married and playing the field. He hid it from her for six months. She found out about his wife through Instagram. Winston just vanished into thin air after that. Now that Ashtin Clarke was a piece of artwork. Out of all her boyfriends, he was the worse. If she was bitter and scorned, it was because of him. Ashtin really put her through some things. She was always stressed out about one thing or another with him. Amarylis could not eat or sleep right. She was losing weight constantly. Her hair was falling out and her edges were almost bald. It took everything in her to hold onto that man. Ashtin was the last straw for her. Maybe it was just a South Carolina thing

Sparkle Riley

at the time. All of them hurt and betrayed her. She gave them her mind, body and soul. Her fragile heart was in the palms of their hands. She got down on her hands and knees and begged Ashtin to stay. He had her out there stalking his trifling ass. Amarylis was slashing his tires and then some. When he ignored her texts and calls, it made her real bizarre and ruthless. Then one day, he just disappeared or ghosted her like what they call it now. Now will Baltimore City be better? Maybe so or maybe not, it was a chance that she was willing to take. There was nothing or no one left in Georgetown South Carolina.

Amarylis picked Baltimore City because she loved their Orioles and Ravens Team. She was thinking about going to Morgan State University. Her Mama Birdie use to talk about the city all the time. Birdie Scott had always wanted to live there. Birdie said Baltimore had good paying jobs. The cost of living was cheaper on the Eastside of Baltimore City. The state had free training programs. You could easily get a place and rent would be based om your income there. Mama made it sound like living in Baltimore City was the American Dream or something. I guess time will only tell, thought Amarylis Scott. It was not like she had

Sparkle Riley

anything else to lose! Birdie was always pumping her head up about it, so it had to be jazzy!

Plus, it was too late to turn back now anyway. It was just jitters. She tried to convince herself that it had to be all right. Amarylis was used to having conversations to herself in her head. Amarylis Scott was fierce and strong. She had seen it all in her years on earth. South Carolina did not love her. Amarylis knew that no one cared if she stayed or left. That is just the way it was. Life can take you through all sorts of changes. You just have to deal with it the best way that you can. It would be nice if she ran into Birdie. When she was little, she would make up all sorts of excuses for her mama. Her mama got lost. Birdie had suffered from amnesia and forgot about her. Her male friend's car broke down. Amar would look out her bedroom window several times a day looking for her mama. Every time the phone rang, she had her little fingers crossed. The doorbell rang and it was always the Mailman or the Avon Lady for Granny Estelle.

Sparkle Riley

Years went by and there was still no mama. That is when the

cold hard truth hit her. Amarylis stopped loving her mama

and went on with her life. Birdie missed all her birthdays,

school plays and her scrapes and scars. Amarylis would not

know what to say to her now. She was an adult now. Woman

to woman, she would have a grudge her.

CHAPTER ONE

At 5pm, Miss. Scott had finally reached her

destination. She was a little tired, but still pumped up! She

made it all the way to Baltimore all by herself. Maybe that is

where her mama ran off to. That would really be something,

running into Birdie Scott in Baltimore. Amarylis was hot and

sweaty waiting for a cab to ride down the famous Baltimore

Street known as The Block. It was hyped up by the glittery

glowing lights of the Strip Clubs and Adult Novelty Stores.

The smells of fried chicken, onions and spices made her

mouth water. Pollock Jimmy's worlds famous smoked

sausage was at the corner. She heard about those polish

Sparkle Riley

sausages drenched in sweet sauerkraut. Men in business suits, looking like lawyers walked in pairs smoking cigars. A haggard looking lady tried to sell her an expired bus pass. She was so persistent and was not taking the word no for an answer. She was out there hustling for her habit. The lady went on to ask for a couple of dollars for a sandwich. "Miss, you got any spare change?" said the Junkie. People were selling loose ones, incense and body oils on every corner. It looked exactly the way that she googled it.

Amarylis used a folded paper towel to wipe her sweaty forehead. As miserable and humid as the weather was, she still managed to put a smile on her face. "I finally made it all the way to B-more! Home of the Old Bay Crabs and the Baltimore Orioles" said Amarylis.

Out of nowhere, a Street Hustler appeared. He had on a black and white bandanna and was smoking a blunt. The smell and smoke of it caused her to cough. The young man smiled and revealed a whole top row of gold teeth. Amarylis

Sparkle Riley

also noticed a spider tattoo under his left eye. He looked a

hot mess with his jeans sagging low and highlighting gray

boxers. He had on a fresh pair of kicks on though. You could

tell that once upon a time, he had seen better days. He still

was not a bad looking dude though. About 6 feet, chiseled

oval face, gray colored eyes and sporting a goatee. He did a

little slow bop as he walked up to her. Amarylis had to laugh

at his corny ass on the low.

"Say little mommy, you ain't waiting on the Number 5

Cedonia is you? That shit might not come for another hour.

You will be better off catching the 35 White Marsh for real.

Where you trying to go anyway Love?" said the Street

Hustler.

He immediately caught the chick's hesitation. He

could dig it because she did not know him like that for real.

He decided to kick it another way then. He thought Amarylis

was cute with her little country looking self. Looking like she

arrived on a horse from some damn farm and shit. She had

real pretty, smooth skin. A little greasy and shiny but it will do. Shorty was about 5ft 8 inches tall. A buck eighty-five pounds of thickness. He closed his eyes and licked his full luscious lips.

"I can see that you ain't from around here. So please, may I have the honor of introducing myself? The name is Dante Jones and I'm a Weedaholic" said Dante and he extended his hand to Amarylis to shake. She immediately took a step back. This was too much for her. She was not about to shake his filthy nasty hands. Besides, she had a bus to catch to Monument and Preston Street. Even when she ignored him, he was still trying to rap to her. Amarylis became very suspicious over the thug that stood in front of her. Amarylis was about to whip out her bottle of pepper spray on him.

Amarylis felt around in her skirt pocket for her wallet. For some reason, something about that thug just did not sit right with her. She fumbled and fumbled in her beige colored

Sparkle Riley

skirt pockets for it. She pulled out Chapstick, Butterscotch candy and a piece of paper. Where in the green meadows is my wallet? It was just in here a few minutes ago, right before Dante pulled up on her. That Street Hustler just pick pocketed me!

Turning her back towards Dante, she started flapping her arms and yelling for someone to help her. "Help, help someone! This man just robbed me. He stole my wallet!" cried Amarylis. Luckily, there was an off-duty officer on the block at the right place and at the right time. A young middle-aged white man approached her and showed her his badge. His name was Officer Bradley. Dante was shocked and scared because he did not even know what she was hollering and screaming about. Amarylis felt an anxiety attack coming on. She started to hyperventilate. It felt as if the whole scene was moving in slow motion. A headache was coming on as her hands started to tremble. Dante was now speechless himself as Officer Bradley spoke.

"Miss, please calm down and tell me exactly what happened? Everything is going to be all right, I promise you. Just take your time and start from the beginning" said Officer Bradley as he tried to comfort her by holding her hand. Amarylis immediately withdrew her hand back with precaution. The Officer immediately turned in the direction of Dante for reasoning of the situation.

"Sir, are you with this young lady or something? What is going on here? I am going to need to see some identification as well" said the Officer. A confused Dontae did not know what to say or do. Obviously, this chick had some major issues. Always the fine ass ones, thought Dante. He decided that maybe he should better speak before he catches an unnecessary charge for some stupid shit. The young lady was just standing there looking crazy like. By now there was a swarm of onlookers surrounding them. Officer Bradley had already started calling for immediate

Sparkle Riley

backup and assistance. Things were spiraling out of control quickly.

"Sir, my name is Dante Jones and I ain't never seen this young lady before in my life. I swear to that. You know I was just trying to rap to little shorty. You know, get the digits and next thing you know she started kirking out on a brotha for no reason. Here's my driver's license Sir" pleaded Dante as he handed him his license. After a few minutes, Amarylis zoned back to reality.

"Officer, I have reason to believe that this thug came up and stole my wallet. He just sort of popped up out of nowhere, too. I don't want to see him get locked up or nothing, I just want my wallet back" said Amarylis, while ready to cry again. Due to the young lady's instability, the Officer had a few more questions for her. If Dante stole her wallet, he would have run off before the police came. Instead, he stood there with a concerned look on his face. Not the look of a thief, that was for sure.

Sparkle Riley

"Miss, you must be terribly mistaken. I do not know nothing about no wallet. I just came over to cop your digits and that was it. Maybe you just misplaced it or something. By looking at you, I could tell that you not from around here. I am not trying to be funny or anything Ma, but you kinda stand out on this street. I'll be happy to help you look for it if you let me" said Dante nicely. That really pissed her off now. Dante took her out of character real quick. His kindness was hiding his true intentions and alternative motives. Dante must think that I am stupid or slow thought Amarylis. If that is the case, then he is in for a big surprise. Amarylis had been with those types before. Pretending to help you while robbing you blind at the same time. Dante got jokes!

"Dante or whatever your name is? Do I look stupid to you? All you men ever do is try to take advantage of us women. Do I look that vulnerable or fragile to you? You just want to use me up and kick me to the curb like all the others. My fiancée just left me at the altar after all I did for him. I trusted him. I believed that he would never hurt me and what did he go and do? Rob me of all my valuables and possessions. I hate all you men, you know that. No offense to you, kind Officer. I am just sick and tired of being treated like trash. Now I stay salty all the time. I want to cuss people out when they say the wrong things to me. I'm just sick of it" said Amarylis. Now the Officer could see the big picture. The young lady was obviously scorned and bitter over some dude. Honestly, I would be too if that happened to me, thought Officer Bradley. Amarylis saw the reluctance to arrest Dante in the Officer's face. She should have figured that all men stick together. Guess the joke was on her then, thought Amarylis. Everybody was looking at her like she was crazy or something.

"So, Officer, now you're going to take his side because he's a man. I am sorry but I hate all men right now, no offense. You have no idea what I have been through. I caught a 15- hour bus ride from Georgetown, South Carolina to start

Sparkle Riley

a new life here in Baltimore City. All I got in this world is the bags on my shoulder and a few dollars. Everything that I worked for is gone. I do not have any family or friends left. I cannot trust anyone half the time. I thought coming to Baltimore would solve all my problems" cried Amarylis. She started crying and was feeling so bad for herself. She was literally breaking down in front of complete strangers. It brought back flashbacks from her wedding day. "Oh God, why me? What have I done for you to punish me so? I am sorry God. I really am for my sins against you. I just need answers as to why, please? You took my Mama Birdie away. Granny Estelle is dead and I'm all alone" cried Amarylis as she dropped to her knees in prayer. As she bowed her head, an unexpected arm hugged her trembling shoulders. That arm belonged to Dante Jones, the Street Hustler.

"Miss, I am sincerely sorry for those horrible events in your life. Baltimore can be a big and dangerous city if you do not know your way around here. Maybe, I could escort you

Sparkle Riley

to Sheppard Pratt for an evaluation. You are deeply troubled dear and can use some professional help" said Officer Bradley. By then, two more Police cars pulled up and two more Officers got out to assist her.

A heavyset black woman approached her and tried to help Amarylis off her knees. Oddly, she did not resist the lady's hand. "Hi, I'm Officer Tanya Wright. Sweetie, do you have your ID on you by chance. I will do everything that I can to help you Miss. Especially if I knew your name" said Officer Wright. Amarylis reached inside her purse for her ID. When she unzipped her purse, her allegedly stolen wallet fell out on the sidewalk. Amarylis was embarrassed now, more than ever. The entire crowd was looking at her like she was crazy or something. Feeling her body tense up, Dante took the lead. He knew that getting the police involved was the last thing that she needed at this time. Putting her in restraints inside of a padded room was not going to help her either.

"Officers, I got this. She is a friend of the family. We have not saw each other since we were in diapers. You have all my information, so it's all good right?" said Dante hoping and praying that the Officers would agree. He had to laugh himself. One minute, Dante claimed that he never saw the chick before and now he knows her. Thank goodness, the Officers did not pick up on that shit. It would be nice if, Amarylis had his back on this one. Amarylis had to admit that she wrongfully blamed him for her past. Something in her, read Dante's mind. This was a stranger looking out for her. Dante was free to go on about his business, yet he stayed with her. Dante had her back no doubt. He had like a shield around her. Amarylis felt as though she should at least combat with him. She decided it was a good idea to join in. At last she has spoken, thought Dante.

"Dante is right. I am sorry for taking up your time Officers. I have been so stressed out lately. I just would rather not bother anybody with my problems. Who wants to

Sparkle Riley

be a burden or a headache? Like a nuisance ant that just refuses to crawl away. But I can assure you Officers, that Dontae has got me covered. I do know this crazy guy now that I have a good look at him. And Officers, if I am feeling overwhelmed again, I will voluntarily check myself in for psychiatric help. I guess we should be heading on over to Dante's place now. Thanks everybody, I appreciate it. Dante, shouldn't we get going? We shouldn't take up any more of their precious time" said Amarylis, adding a little extra Southern charm. Dante knew that she was doing the most because she reached up and caressed his cheek. Dante was taken by surprise at her touch. It sent chills through his body like an electricity.

Now that the coast was clear, Dante and Amarylis had a chance to exchange a few words. Dante still did not like the fact that Amarylis called him out as a thief. Dante was opposed to racial profiling and biased stereotypes. Although he fit the description of a Street Hustler, he was far from it.

Not even close to it, but that was none of Amarylis' business. He was living a complicated life. Now, he was worrying about what he just walked into. He foolishly and willingly agreed to look after a crazy chick, right in front of the Police. Now Amarylis Scott was his responsibility and he knew that he was screwed. But he knew that he could never just walk away from her either. Amarylis had been to hell and back. He understood why she had a bad attitude now. Dante did not want to be the next bad guy on her list. Either way, he was in a jam! Dante damn sure was not taking her back to his crib, because he had a whole wifey at home. He and her were trying to work things out at home. Every time he tried to do good, something bad happened. He just keeps getting caught up in situations that are not good for him. No matter how hard he tried he could not get out of it. He loved Laia, he just could not get his act together. No matter how hard he tried. He was always lying to her and keeping secrets from her. He knew he was dead wrong for trying to cop some girl's digits like that.

But now he had a problem on his hands. He looked at his phone and Laia called him like a hundred times. Laia was just overprotective of her man. Laia was in love with him, plain and simple. He will have to do a lot of explaining to do that was for sure.

Laia would have to go on the back burner again. But only for one night. By tomorrow Amarylis Scott would be out of his hair. He would be sending the country peach on her merry little way. He was going to do whatever it took to get her on the right track before he vanished. If she traveled all the way to Baltimore by herself, she must have thought this through. It would be totally insane to go out on a limb like that without a plan.

Amarylis was still trying to process her new situation. Here is this Street Hustler willing to drop everything to help her. She accused him of stealing her wallet and he is still standing here. He probably had Weed to sell. He probably had babies at home that needed him. He probably had an ankle monitor on his leg. What if he was on probation or something? Amarylis did not want to be the reason that he went back to jail.

Amarylis did what she did best and that was to focus on the negative. She was just set in her ways. Every guy wanted to steal something from her. At least all the guys back home did. Amarylis remembered countless times when cash was missing from her wallet. Those guys in South Carolina really did her dirty. That is why she freaked out so bad over her wallet. But anybody can make a mistake. Dante was innocent just this once. Amar knew he had more tricks up his sleeve because they always do. Amarylis had not met a man yet that was not trying to manipulate her in some way. This little Street Hustler is not slick because I am hip to the game. Trust and believe that, she thought to herself.

Sparkle Riley

Dante was worried to death now. He kept checking his watch because he was late. Laia was going to kill him. He was a whole hour late because of Amarylis. He could never just leave her on the block like that. Dante had to think quick. He prayed silently to himself. It had worked for him in the past, so why not now. "Dear God, please get me out of this. I promised my girl that I was going to do right by her, if she took me back. God can you babysit Amarylis because I can't right now" pleaded Dante.

Amarylis had just walked out of a liquor store with a brown paper bag in her hand. All she could think about was getting her buzz on and kicking it with the Street Hustler for the night. She sure could use a friend to talk to. It was a big city with flashing lights. Dante could even be her tour guide. Amarylis wanted to go to the Inner Harbor, she heard it was lit. He could be her bodyguard while she checked out Monument Street. She liked all those fancy colored wigs in them Korean Hair Stores. Oh, and the Northeast Market for

Sparkle Riley

them famous chicken boxes and western fries smothered in seasoned salt and hot sauce. Her mouth was just a watering for a tall cup of half and half. There was nothing like B-more's half lemon and half tea drink. That was the way Birdie always described it. Amarylis always wanted to go to a concert in the park. Druid Hill Park was known for just that. The free cultural and musical Afram was the hottest place to be under the sun. Summer concerts there in the park attracted singers and artists from around the world. Birdie used to mention their Reggae festivals too. She heard that was off the chain too. Something like what fresh Peach Tea from her hometown was to her.

Amarylis could not help but notice the worried look on Dante's face. She took a big sip from her brown alcohol bag. Amaryllis was getting worried now. Flashbacks of her past exes were haunting her. She hoped that he was not trying to renege on his promise to her. She did not have time for the okie-dokie. She has been through hell and back. She was

Sparkle Riley

hungry and tied as a mule. It had been a hectic day. If he acts right, she might even let him hit it tonight. Amarylis wanted Dante. She desired his body, warmth and slobbery kisses all over her body. Amarylis took another hard swallow of her brown bag liquor. The alcohol made her hot and horny. Amarylis had not slept with anyone in a long time. She had to admit that Dante was looking hell a fine to her. He was hood on the outside, but sugary sweet on the inside. His gold fronts were dazzling. That sexy goatee was calling her name. The alcohol was clouding her judgement to the point of no control. Go get it girl, thought Amarylis to herself.

"Say Partner, I guess I should properly introduce myself. Especially, since you and I are going to be kicking it later. My name is Miss. Amarylis Scott from Georgetown, South Carolina. My Mama Birdie is missing in action and my Granny is dead. I am twenty-seven, a Scorpio and I do not take no shit from nobody. I am not out here looking for no man because I don't got time for all that. I am too young to

Sparkle Riley

be tied down to one guy. I got my place and you better have your own shit too. I don't do the shacking up thing, kay" said Amarylis while snapping her fingers.

Dante was saved by the bell because the number 35 bus was pulling up to the corner where they were standing at. He quickly started grabbing on Amarylis arm. He tried to shove her on the bus but failed. Amarylis stood right there fussing with her hands on her hips and not moving an inch She was pointing in his face, cussing and rolling her eyes.

"Fool, have you lost your every lasting mind? Get your nasty ass hands off me, Dante. This is not how you treat a real woman. These city girls might like that rough shit but Amarylis Scott is not the one Partner" yelled Amarylis.

Dante started cracking up. Amarylis was geeking because she was a little bit tipsy! This chick was an undercover ghetto city girl. Where was that sweet peachy charm that only the country girls had? He did not have time to be fooling with her like that. She was getting all loud and

Sparkle Riley

ignorant making a big old scene. And for what, thought

Dante. If her butt made them miss this bus, it was on. They

had been waiting over an hour for it.

CHAPTER 2

"Little mommy, we need to hop on this bus for real. I

ain't got time for your mess now. You on my time now. I

agreed to help you, now let me do it. I ain't got no money for

no fucking hack. Catch this bus or walk to Monument

Street!" yelled Dante.

Oh no this fool did not just try to throw shade at her,

thought Amarylis. She was still standing there holding her

heavy ass bags for crying out loud. Dante could have at least

been a gentleman about and offer to carry her bags for her.

He most definitely was not getting any now. Amarylis

thought to herself, Dante has lost his mind. They were both

standing there arguing like two crazy fools when the doors

swung open on the bus. The Bus Driver just needed to know

if they were getting on or not. The other passengers were

getting agitated by their inconveniences. "Are you lovebirds riding or not?" asked the Bus Driver. They both kept arguing, so the number 35 bus just pulled right off.

"Shit Amar, we missed the damn bus because of you showing out. You in Baltimore now, if you want something done, you better ask for it. Closed mouths don't get fed up in the big city, Gal. Do I look like a Fortune teller Ma? How was I supposed to know that you wanted me to carry your stupid bags? I would not carry them anyway. Your butt my zap out on me again. You are really a piece of artwork. You been in Baltimore for an hour and you're already cutting up" said Dante while shaking his head. He was hot and angry over this chick right here. Amar ain't nothing but trouble. Dante wished he never got involved with her. Seeing and feeling his frustrations caused her to react on it. Amarylis realized what she had done and tried to console Dante. She sat her duffle bags down and walked over to him. Dante was pacing the sidewalk and mumbling to himself. "What in the hell have I gotten myself into?" he said.

"Alright Dante, I screwed up. Bite me. The bus is gone and there is nothing we can do about it now. Look, we can flag down that hack thing that you were talking about. I will help you pay for it. Just help me get settled into my room please. I had a little too much to drink. After that Dante you are free to go your way and I will go mine. I am sorry for making you late for whatever you do. I do not know if you work, sell drugs or steal cars. You want to get some carry out first?" said Amarylis. She felt bad for poor Dante. He probably needed that little job.

Dante wanted to be mad at Amar, but he just could not do it. Laia was already going to chop his head off for being late and not calling or texting. Carry out did sound nice and it was a nice summer night. He had enough in his wallet for their hack and something to eat, so why not? Besides Monument and Preston Street was not a safe place for a

Sparkle Riley

young lady like her. He was sincerely concerned for her safety. Amarylis was a stranger, that he knew was not right for him. At least not in his current situation. It was just bad timing. He did not feel like going home to fight all night with Laia. Tonight, he was not listening to Laia's nagging and complaining. He walked up to Amar and put his arm around her shoulder and told her that it was all good. One night on the town was not going to do any damage. Besides Amar had the look of seduction in her eyes. It was that look that he never saw from wifey.

"I know that I shouldn't be doing this. Even though, I do not really know you like that, I feel like I have known you my whole life, Amarylis. My mom is having financial problems and was looking for someone to rent out one of her rooms. I think that would be much better and safer than renting out some room. After we grab a bite to eat, we can stop in and check it out. My Moms is cool people, you'll love her!" said Dante with a smile.

"I don't know what to say Dante. We like literally just met today and already you want me to meet your mom and move in with her just like that. It is a good idea, I will admit. But I need to think about that one. I should not be making any decisions while tipsy" said Amarylis. It was an offer that she should not be refusing. But this was just too soon. It was too much for her. Dante had good intentions, but it just was not right time. Amarylis made her decision.

"I appreciate that, I really do Dante. But I should at least give my place a try first. I hope you understand that. You and I can still hang out. I still need a bodyguard and a handyman, if you're free" said Amarylis with a smile. It was strange because her mind told her to say no while her heart said to trust Dante. It was so weird and new to her at the same time.

Dante took a fake gulp and balled up his sweaty hands to make a fist in his jean pocket. He secretly hoped that Amar said yes. His mother could use the companionship, especially

Sparkle Riley

after tragically losing his only sister. He decided that it was best not to be persistent about it. The night was young and so were they. This was Amar's first night in the big city, it was about to get lit. Might as well show her a good time then. Dante knew of a perfect place to take her. Ty's Fish and Chips about three blocks away. He had the best Lake Trout and BBQ Chicken in the city. It was a little lounge with a nice dance floor. The bar was lit. Amar was going to love it.

"Check this out, I got you. I want to take you to this little hole in my city. Food so good it be denting shit. We can kick it, get our drink on if you down for it, Amar. I'm telling you this place is off the chain' said Dante.

Amar decided to go. Only because she wanted to fill her contact list up. Dante is not going to be the only guy that I mess with like that. Shoot, I have never been the clingy, thirsty type. I am never sitting around waiting on no guy to hit me up. What I look like chasing some guy down and blowing up his phone? I will never be wifey material. But as a grown woman, I still can go out and get my freak on. I been there and done that already plenty of times. I can have great sex and leave a man's bed right after I am done. It just simply does not pay to be some guy's ride or die no more. Nobody wants to be loyal and faithful these days. I had mad men that I would die for, shit on me and left me for the next chick. I still do not know what I did wrong to be honest. Now, I am just a young lady, who is into random hook-ups and flings. Back in South Carolina, I did me. I made sure that I got mines, too. Shacking up with a few of them was her thing back home. At the end of the day, I was left carrying my bags all by myself. I am trying not to do that all over again. Those thoughts were getting into her head again.

"Why not, right? After that you can drop me off at my crib, that is if I do not get a ride at the spot. Who knows? Me and you are just cool Dante, alright. You can do your thang because I am damn sure going to do mine. Just because you are taking me to Ty's, just know that I do not have to go

Sparkle Riley

home with you. I did not come all the way up to Baltimore not to live my best life now. I am going to live it up. I'm single and nobody's messy baby mama, come on now" said Amar.

Amar recited those words a hundred times until she started to believe them. You know get at a few random guys numbers that was popping to her. They all had to work and drive and have they own crib. Sis was not putting out for no loser. Like take Dante for example, his behind did not even drive for real. Amar was not into encounters with men on foot or carrying around bus passes. He was not getting any from her. If he had a couple of dollars, he might could be cool. At least for the time being, thought Amar with a smirk on her face.

Dante was really digging Amar's style. It was sort of Gangsta and sweet at the same time. She kept it 100 right off the bat. He had a girl anyway, so the heck with her. Amar

Sparkle Riley

looked like she could handle her own shit. A real classy

bossy thing. Ooh wee, thought Dante to himself!

CHAPTER 3

"Oh, I'm down for that alright. I do not need no drama

in my life right now. I just need a down cool like girl to chill

with from time to time, know what I mean. No strings

attached and no headache. I guess you country girls stay

winning then, huh?" said Dante.

On that note, Amar had to flip the script on that fool.

Never in her life had she been a part of anybody's group. She

always did her own thing and never had to answer to nobody

and never would. What did this fool mean by you country

girls? I guess I got to break it down for Dante Jones, then. I

am not going to let him get one up over me now, thought,

Amarylis.

"You know what Dante. I was going to cuss you out. But I am not fin to let you ruin my first night in the city, you know that. You do not know nothing about me or what I been through, kay. I do not care about you at all, Dante Jones. I am just your lady friend for the minute. When and if I need something, I expect you to come through with it. Because I got it like that. I am not bumming nothing from you because you going to cop that for me. Especially, if you are going to be hitting me up behind your girl's back. If you going to be in my DM's, you got to pay my cellphone bill. And if you cannot please me Dante, then you will have another problem. Partner you will be kicking out some cash to buy me a new cellphone! Am I right? Because baby it is what it is?" said Amarylis.

Damn, he thought in his mind. Little shorty goes hard on a brother like him. She read my mind and shit like no other chick. I got to agree with that. Wait until my homeboys hear about my new little shorty all the way from South

44

Carolina. She cute, real ghetto with a bad ass attitude. This Southern cutie is not playing no games. Nah, I would never disrespect no chick like her, like that. She is not no bottom hoe. Amarylis is just ratchet and mean as a Rottweiler, thought Dante.

CHAPTER 4

"Then let us do the thang then shorty. I got you. Ain't going to be no feeling involved or none of that shit. Girl, you might make me get addicted to your mentality fast. I am digging how you carry yourself" said Dante. He lightly grabbed her arm and led her down the block to Ty's joint. He was hoping to run into one of his boys there too. He wanted to show off his new dime piece.

The parking lot of Ty's was packed with cars. Music was blasting. People was dancing and smoking grass in the parking lot. They were just a bunch of young people having a good time together. And ain't nothing wrong with that, thought Dante.

Sparkle Riley

As they walked in, Amar was already locking eyes at a fine-looking brother in the corner. He drove that 2019 Black Acura with the tinted windows, that she was peeping out in the parking lot. He was just her type too. He had a couple of dollars, no doubt. She could tell by the way he was standing there profiling. Amar could not help but stare at that big thick print in his gray sweatpants. Amar did not have no shame in her game and neither did he. He was over there cheesing too. He pointed at Dante on the low. Amar gave a wink to let him know what time it was. When he grabbed his big wood thing, Amar licked her lips seductively to let him know she was down for anything. Yup, anything goes tonight.

Dante was too busy trying to find them a table, to peep what Amar was up to. He was kind of upset that none of his boys were there. He really wanted them to meet his new lady friend. You know, show her off a little. Make their mouths water for his new Southern Peachy thing. As usual when you need them, they are nowhere to be found. He wanted the

Sparkle Riley

perfect spot for them. Not too close to the bar or by the dance floor. He really wanted to talk to her and get to know her more. He figured that she probably wanted to get more acquainted with him too. At least he hoped she did. He thought Amar was still behind him, so he said "Amar, how about over here" He was surprised that she was not trailing behind in his footsteps. But she was nowhere to be found. He scratched his sweaty forehead. Since he was a little hot from obvious reasons, he took off his bandana, while thinking to himself. Dang, Shorty is it like that? We ain't even been here for a hot second and you already up in a new chump's face. I must be real invisible to her and dude. I am starting to think that this shit ain't for me, for real. Now that I think about it, I must look real stupid standing here all by myself. Everybody seen us come in this joint together, now some other chump is sucking on her neck. My lil shorty is a freak for real, thought Dante.

Amar and dude were already planning to go to a motel, by the looks of it. But not until he hooked her up with some job leads first. Amar was all about getting hers. His brother owned an Assisted Living Facility on Pennsylvania Avenue. Charles said he would hook her up because his brother needed an assistant. Judging by his sexual needs and that ring on his finger, it was a win win for the her and Charles.

Amarylis did not mean to leave Dante hanging like that, but she had to do what she had to do. She wanted to get laid but with benefits. Sis was all about making her paper. She just had to politely tell Dante that she needed to take a raincheck on dinner. But on second thought, forget him. He already knew what time it was. Still though, she walked over to rap to him for a second.

"Dante, check this out. Me and you going to have to kick it another day. Dude just got what I need. A little nuddy and some money. I just found me a gig to get my money on point. Write your number down or something if you want to.

Sparkle Riley

But hurry up about it, do not mess up my shot though. I wouldn't do you dirty like that, so I'd appreciate the same thing, kay" said Amar. Shorty was on some new shit for real. He had never met a girl quite like her before. Dante walked over to the bar to get a pen and something to write on. As he was walking back, he felt his phone vibrating. He already knew it was Laia. He tried to turn his phone off, but Amar caught it first.

"See this that shit that I be talking about right here. Dante, your girl got your butt on a ball and chain already. Y'all not even married yet. That is real stupid on your part. That is why I do not want no man Dante. You better handle that shit before it gets out of control. Dante, you do not owe her an explanation either. You do not have no curfew Partner. You are a grown man! Look at Charles over there, that man is out here handling his business. He got on a ring and still do what he do. Charles got his cellphone's ringer on. See that is what I be trying to tell you. Tell your girl to buzz off Dante.

Remember no explanations are ever needed. You better than us. Nobody better not be blowing up my phone like that. Charles, I know you feel me on that one Partner. Go on and tell him what is good? You better go get you some on the side. I thought all you B-more fellas got down like that. I am at a loss for words Partner. Boy bye" said Amar in tears. Her and Charles were really cracking up over there. Dante felt real stupid now. The joke was on him, so he had to play it off. He had an image to protect. He was not trying to go out looking like no fool.

"Oh, Cousin! Did you think that she was my girl? No sir, that chick is not my cup of tea. I got better taste in women than that. Amar is just one of my thots. Yo, just to let you know, Amar is not even close to being my girl. So, do not be thinking you got one up on me, kay" said Dante. They were dying laughing, but then Amar had a tight face. He was so adamant about her not being his girl and it was driving her

Sparkle Riley

bananas. Charles was just enjoying their show. He turned his attention to Takia,

"Amar, what kind of country name is that? I thought you said your name was Takia. Is your name Amar or Takia? What y'all is? Some freaks and shit" said Charles. Charles had seen it all tonight!

"Partner don't drink the Kool-Aid if you do not know the flavor. Because we both know that your name ain't no Charles either. Like I said before I been around guys like you my whole life. No man can put no wool over my eyes no more. That shit ain't fin to go down like that. Dante, you city boys ain't shit!" said Amar. She felt way by his hurtful words. Is that what he really thought of her? Amar was in her feelings because she did not expect him to say all that. Maybe Dante was just mad and jealous. Yeah, that had to be it, she thought. Just like that her and what's his name was out, with no explanation?

Sparkle Riley

Dante caught a hack home about an hour after Amar left. He got let out about a block from where he lived by choice. Instead of knocking on his apartment door, he decided to just sleep in the laundry room. He did not want to get Laia started at 3 am in the morning. Laia told him that if he is going to be late, he ain't coming in his own apartment. Now that he thought about that shit, it was real crazy on his part. How he let his girl put him out his own place? He was the only one working and paying all the bills. He paid their cellphone bills, the rent and the electric. Shit, he even paid for the car note and the insurance. Laia snapped and took his keys one time before because she caught him checking out another girl at the mall. Now he had to catch the bus and hack now. Laia took his car right from him like a child. I must be real delusional to put up with that mess. All their shit was is in my name too. Man, my girl ain't even all that for real for real, thought Dante to himself. He just found an old raggedy folding chair in the corner and just decided to make

Sparkle Riley

the best of it. He was tired anyway. His neck was all crooked and his back was killing him. Dante decided that he was going to let Laia's have it when the sun came up. It did, with Laia standing right there with her hands on her hips, talking smack first thing in the morning. He took a good look at her and Amar. Without a doubt, Amar was prettier than Laia, just meaner.

"Nicca, get your nasty black ass up! Where your dusty ass been at all night? Are you screwing that nappy head thot from Mondawmin mall, huh? Let me smell your drawers Dante!" yelled Laia. She was kicking him in the leg and smacking the shit out of him. The other tenants heard all that ruckus and came down to signify. You know first thing black people going to do is pull their phones out. Everybody got to be on Facebook live for clout.

Dante did not want to put his hands on her because his mama raised him better than that. He had a little sister, so he knew how to treat a woman. Besides he and Laia were over.

Sparkle Riley

That shit right there was done. He could always go back home to his mama. Maybe even crash at Amar's crib for a minute. Just until he got shit together.

"Laia, what are you talking about? I was chilling at my mama's house. Why is that any of your concern? We ain't never going to get married at the rate. What is up with all these questions? I cannot go out. I cannot see my mama. You do not want me to look at other girls. Am I your prisoner or your man, Laia? This right here, ain't working for me no more. All we do is argue and fight over petty ass shit. Laia I'm out" yelled Dante. Laia started pulling on his arm and crying. She did not want her man to leave like that, especially in front of an audience.

"Wait, where do you think you're going? We need to continue this conversation in private, Dante. Let us just take this upstairs to our apartment. We don't need these nosey ass neighbors all up in our business like that" said Laia. But Dante clearly was not trying to hear that.

Sparkle Riley

"Nah Laia, you made it their business, by putting on this show in front of them. You like dogging me out on Facebook and Instagram all the time They videotaped this whole mess that you got us in. I don't got nothing to say to you right now. I need some space to clear my head. So, if you'll excuse" said Dante as he brushed passed her. Laia was just too dramatic. Her social media accounts were the other reasons for their failing relationship. Laia put all their business on there for likes. She would rather talk to strangers than to talk to him. Her Facebook friends were always giving her bad relationship advice. They were all salty and bitter and a tad bit jealous. But she was stupid enough to ask and trust their opinion. Laia just had too much time on her hands. She did not want to work or go take up a trade. All she did was worry about what he was doing all day long. That too, was driving him away.

Amar was on to a good thing back there. Being in a relationship was overrated. Take Amar for example, she was

Sparkle Riley

carefree and living her best life. She did not have to answer to no one. She can come and go as much as she pleases. That Laia was giving him a headache. She was too jealous and insecure. They were acting like an old married couple. They did not go out on dates or nothing. All Laia wanted to do was watch music videos or reality tv. He wanted to rip those mink fake eyelashes off. They were thicker than his broom bottom. He was sick of her fur slides. Them things were so ghetto and tacky. Laia whined about getting a dog until he got for her. Now she does not want to clean up his poop or nothing. I come home from a hard day at work to step in his shit. Laia was letting herself go and everything. Living with her was one of the worse decisions that he made so far. He did not want to listen to his mama or his homeboy. Now he was stuck between a rock and a hard place. The question was how was he going to get out of it? His place did not feel like home anymore. His bathroom was decorated in pink butterflies. Laia hung her wigs over the shower curtain. He did not have

Sparkle Riley

a drawer or closet to put his clothes in. Why am I even there, thought Dante? I just pay the bills up in this joint, lol.

Dante had Amar on his mind for some reason. He hoped that she was alright because she went to a motel with some random dude. Her first night in Baltimore City and she was already thotting. Dante figured that them dudes must have hurt her real bad to be that loose and easy. He was not her man, but he was still going to roast her butt for that. Going home with random dudes was something that ugly chicks did. Amarylis was too cute for that. She was a good woman with a good head on her shoulders. She just caught a few bad apples in her basket. He felt his phone vibrating and at first, he was not going to answer it, but decided to anyway.

"Who the fuck is this?" said Dante even though he already knew who it was. This was an everyday thing for them now. He and Laia been together on and off for almost three years now. They would always break up and then get back together. His mama told him not to move in with that crazy girl, but he did it anyway.

"Bae, I'm sorry for fucking you up. I just love you Dante. You and I got a good thang going. We have been together three years strong. I know you got bitches on you Boo. I just know that I got me the finest man in Baltimore City. I just got jealousy issues. Dante, you all out here fine as hell. So, it really is your fault. Just come on home Bae, I got my food stamps today. We got a son together and everything, Dante" cried Laia.

"What son Laia? You mean our Pitbull Rex. I know you ain't pregnant because I use rubbers. If I did not buy them myself, then that would be a different story. Your thirsty ass might try to poke tiny holes in the rubbers. But for real though Laia, this is not working for me at all. And no, it's not no other chick in the picture" lied Dante. There was someone in the picture, he was just in denial.

CHAPTER 5

Sparkle Riley

Dante was walking to the bus stop when his phone rang. He was hoping that it was Amar. When he saw the name wifey on his screen, he hit decline quick. He was to stay at his mother's house for a few days. His mama was not going to be happy about this one. She told him to stop running from his problems and to handle his business. Seconds later, it was wifey calling again.

Laia thought it was funny for real. She was not worrying about it because he always said that when he was a little bit mad. Laia knew that Dante's behind was not going anywhere. He did not have anywhere else to go really but to his mama's house anyway. His butt was twenty-eight years old for crying out loud. He was too old to be a mama's boy. Laia was determined to get him to talk to her. Dante is so childish and immature, she thought. He loved being difficult. He will get over it, he always does. Laia was believing that up until he dropped a bomb on her. She felt her heart stop

Sparkle Riley

beating and she felt like she could not breathe no more. Dante had never said that before. Oh shit, thought Laia.

"Look we got three more months in our lease. I am going to put in a sixty-day notice for our place. I advise you to start looking for a place to stay. You can keep my car because I never cared for it anyway. They can repossess the Jetta for all I care. I ain't even want to get that car Laia, you did. I wanted the Lexus for the same price. You made me not get it on purpose. You said I would be pulling to many bitches in it. Man, you really got me fucked up in that overpriced lease for it too. I am struggling trying to keep up with the car payments and car insurance. It ain't like you can contribute anything. You want to call all the shots though. I am backed the fuck up now. I got to keep getting your hair and nails done. My credit is fucked up and all this shit is in my name. I did not even want that stupid, bougie ass dog either. That mean ungrateful motherfucker eat better than me. My stupid ass work two jobs for y'all and I got to eat canned

Spam for dinner!" yelled Dante. Amar was started to rub off on him in a good way.

Dante could hear Laia laughing but he was dead serious. He was about to board the number 5 Cedonia Bus to his mama's house. His Mama, Siarra lived on Sinclair Lane. He did not even call her to give her a heads up. He knew she was going to lay him out again. Laia started zapping out as soon as he answered.

"Dante, you ain't even got to act like that. You trying to make something out of nothing. We had a little spat, so what? That is what couples do in long term relationships Dante. It is not that serious. Just take a time out and get back home on time. It is not like I am asking for no fucking engagement ring. Even though I deserve one, I am like pressing the issue every day. I am waiting patiently so give me a little credit. If this is about dinner, I can fix that. I did not appreciate what you said about our dog either. How are you going to compare yourself to our baby like that? But,

Sparkle Riley

since you are being petty as usual, I guess I can try to fry

bologna instead of Spam. How's that?" said Laia.

Dante was about to cuss Laia out, but then a text came

through. It was Amar. He was so excited that he just hung up

Laia. He did not want the people on the bus all up in his

business anyway. Laia was still talking when the phone went

click. His gray eyes were glued to his phone's screen. It was

Amarylis Scott!

Dante could not believe the words on his screen. Amar

was texting him about needing some Maxi-pads. She wanted

him to go to Rite Aid and then bring them up to her job for

her. He never even bought them for his mama or sister, go

rest her soul. This chick must of lost her mind if she thought

he'd do some crazy shit like that. Amar was not his girl. As a

matter a fact, he did not even have no girl. She should have

asked tall ass Charles, he hit last night.

Dante was looking at all the shelves. It was a thousand pads on the shelf. Some of them Maxi Birds could fly! They had wings and everything. All them came in different sizes. It was all too confusing, luckily someone tapped him on the shoulder. Somebody with a heavy hand. He turned around ready to cuss some lady out that was standing behind him. Dante because was so frustrated. He could not wait to come face to face with boxer hands. When he turned around, he blacked out and saw stars.

"Cuzzo, what you on your period now? Laia got you out here buying pads and shit now. Boy you is whipped whipped! Why can't her lazy butt do it herself? She ain't got shit else to do all day. But I guess it's still good because at least you know she ain't pregnant!" said Jermaine.

Embarrassed as hell, he had to have a comeback. This is not how he wanted his homeboy to find out about Miss. Amarylis. It was too late though. Plus, he needed a ride because it was so hot out. He was not trying to kick out no money for a hack. Jermaine was his homeboy and he had wheels. He knew his mama was going to have her hand out for a couple of dollars for staying there. He knew that Siarra was not playing that broke mess. If you stay, you must pay. No ifs, ands or buts.

"Whatever Bruh! Can you drop me off at my friend's job over on Pennsylvania Avenue? Who you got in your ride Cousin? I just need to drop this off to my homegirl and then I need a ride up to my mama's house. I wish I would have taken your advice a long time ago. I broke it off with Laia, man. I am quitting the jobs that she got me, too. Her sister got me one and her Cousin Shayla got me the other one. You remember her fine ass Cousin Shay? If I were the dog that she always accused me of being, I would have had my shot at shorty, by now. But I do not roll like that. Just think I never cheated on her crazy tail. I had plenty of opportunities. She really messed up this time, Jermaine. Laia will never find another brother like me" said Dante.

Sparkle Riley

Jermaine did not pay him no attention. Dante was known to say one thing and then do another. Everybody in Baltimore City knew he was not leaving that girl. They had too much history together. Jermaine knew that it was better to mind his business. He did not want Laia turning on him, too. The last thing he wanted was bad blood between him and Dante over her. He knew he did some things in the past that he was not proud of. Getting in the middle of their conflict would air out his past dirty laundry. At the end of the day, no chick was worth driving a wedge between them.

"Man, shut the fuck up. Your ass will be back by tomorrow. Everybody in Baltimore knows that. So, you got you a little friend now. I hear that and it is about time too. But if you are serious this time, you know I got you Bruh. You know I stay riding thots in my ride Dante. I got Kera and her ghetto ass Cousin Tiana in my ride. You know they stay tricking for Weed. You trying to hang out with us or not?" said Jermaine.

Sparkle Riley

Dante turned his homeboy down talking about he had to do something for his moms. That was only partially true though. He also wanted to kick it with Amar again. Charles tall ass had to go. Besides, that man had a whole wife at home. He probably got a few children at home too. Why play the field, if you got a woman at home, thought Dante?

"Another time Bruh. I got to get in my mama's good graces again. You know that she is going to throw the book at me with I told you so. I am going to need to get a job and save up to get some wheels and everything. You been to any auctions lately or know anybody selling a car for cheap? I need some wheels, know what I mean" said Dante. Dante had a lot of things to do honestly. For the first time in his life he felt incomplete like he had been missing something all his life. It could be something or someone, who knows?

As they approached Jermaines's ride, Kera got out of the front seat to ride in the back with her cousin. They were not dating as far as he knew. He heard about her thirsty

Sparkle Riley

cousin a long time ago. Tiana was an East Baltimore freak. Immediately as soon as he got in, Tiana was ready and willing to shoot her shot with him.

"Hey Dante! Sorry about your loss. Laia just posted y'alls break-up on Facebook live. Yo, she up there saying that you was cheating and beating on her. Did you even know that Laia was two months pregnant too" joked Kera. She lived for the drama, so this made her day.

Now thirsty Tiana was ready to go in for the kill. She had been trying to hook up with Dante forever. Tiana has been eyeing him since the moment he and Laia got together. Tiana was an airhead but a fine ass one. Since Laia wanted to take it there, maybe he should go there with her. Laia kept accusing him of cheating, so why not do it? Amar was living her best life and getting hers. That little thing that Laia did had his mind playing tricks on him. All his personal business was all over social media. He knew that everybody was going to be hating on him. Social media was going to drag his butt to hell for Laia's lies. All the chicks were going to side with her lies anyway. He was going to be roasted either way. The chicks were going to be blowing her timeline up with, Girl Dante is a dog. He ain't no good Girl. You need to put him on child support for your dog. Blah blah blah, he thought to himself.

"You is a single sexy man now. You are free of your chains Love. Why not enjoy yourself while you got the chance? Dante because we all know you going to run back to her yellow ass. That reminds me, I should be taking bets on you as we speak. I can sure use the money. Come on out to Eldorado's Strip Club with us. Our little Cousin Fantasy is the Star of that joint. I know you're tired of looking at that skinny, not butt having Laia all day" said Tiana.

Dante could not deny that he was tempted. He did not have enough cash for the Champagne Room though. Maybe his friends could hook him up. Besides Amar probably had plans already herself. It could not hurt to let loose for a

Sparkle Riley

change. Wait, have I ever been to a Gentleman's Club, thought Dante? Being in a committing relationship was for the birds. Since he been with Laia he had missed out on all the fun! Dante was smiling as they turned right on Pennsylvania Avenue to get to Amar's job.

"Yo, it's right over there, thanks. Y'all know what, count me in for tonight. I'll be right back, let me holler at somebody for a minute" said Dante as he got out of the car with the Rite Aid bag real quick. He was pumped now. One was because he was finally going out with friends and the other was seeing Amarylis again.

Dante walked up the deteriorating wheelchair ramp to the facility. The smell of stale urine burned his nostrils. You could hear an elderly man banging his cane against his window while screaming to be let out. It looked like a rat infested, hell hole. Cardboard was taped onto the broken glass windows. Trashcans were overturned on the side of the facility. Rats were scurrying all around munching on leftover

Sparkle Riley

scraps. It was sad that those old people had to take their last breath in that dump. You would think that the Health Department would have gave them a citation by now. Amar opened the door as soon as she saw him, she started smiling. Dante was the first guy to do that for her. Dante was scoring big points in her book. Amar decided that she would never tell him though. Dante figured that she must have saw him walking up. Shorty opened the door so fast, that he never even got a chance to ring the doorbell.

"Hey Amar, how are you? I hope I got the right pads for you. Can I come in for a second? Do you have a minute? I know you are busy. I just thought I'd ask" said Dante as he was looking at the ground instead of at her. He was shuffling a beer can with his feet while trying not to look in her eyes. They were not even together like that. He was already feeling guilty for going out with his friends later. It was Amar's eyes. She was so alluring that he could not resist looking at

Sparkle Riley

her even if he tried. Dante could not describe the fireworks between them.

She was starring past his dreamy gray eyes out into the vehicle with the chicks in it. She wanted to know who they were? Where are they going? Amar was going to catch a cab home but when she saw two chicks in the back, she changed her mind. Might as well, ride with Dante and his girlfriend, laughed Amar to herself. Dante was so busy avoiding eye contact that he had not noticed the bags on her shoulders. When he saw her bags, his heart skipped a beat. What in the hell is wrong with me, he thought? He hoped that Amar was not leaving so soon. He really wanted to get to know her a little bit more. It was not just physically it was mentally and emotionally as well. He wanted to get to know her spiritual too.

"Where are you going all packed up, Sunshine? You just got here. I never had a chance to be your tour guide or bodyguard. We still got to eat at Ty's" said Dante sadly. He was rambling on and on. He never noticed her frowning up at Jermaine's car.

Amarylis was ready to set it off up in there. Dante reminded her of one of her exes. That bastard had a whole girlfriend at home and did not care to tell her. Her anxiety attacks were coming on. Amar could not breathe no more because of her exe's betrayal. Come on and pull yourself together Amarylis. Dante is not your ex she whispered under her breath. Amarylis Scott pull yourself together for sexy bedroom eyes standing in front of you, Girl.

"Go to hell Dante. So, what do you expect me to be, huh? A third wheel for you and your girlie. I thought you and her broke up Dante. What are you being so nice to me for? You got the nerve to act like you care about me! I hate you and this job. Charles cut me off, kay. He said I better lose his number. I know that his brother is going to fire me. Well guess what? I quit right now Dante. I cannot do this no more. It is a lady in there that reminds me of my Granny Estelle, kay. She smells like Bengay and walks just like her. When she asked if I wanted a piece of Butterscotch Candy, I totally lost it, Kay. Just take me home and I ain't riding with your pretty little girlfriend either" cried Amar.

Now Dante was not ready for that right here. He believed some of it what she was saying but not all of it. Amar had real tears when she was crying. He believed that Amar missed her Grandma. He could see that one of the residents reminded her of her Grandma Estelle and that was not the issue he had. But she was expressing a little streak of jealously over the girls in the car. That made him blush, too. Now she was doing too much. Imagine if that was really Laia or his girl. He would be in a tough situation. It would be a hard decision. Dante knew that he could never leave her like that. Dante wondered, what kind of men did she deal with, back in South Carolina? Amar was still broken up over them that was for sure. Dante knew why it was such a huge ordeal for her now. Her mama left her all alone and her grandma

Sparkle Riley

died unexpectantly. All her ex-boyfriends dogged her out. He had to admit that made him see her in a whole new light. He had compassion and empathy for her now. He vowed to never to a name on her shit list of men. It was a known fact that no one can completely heal without closure. You can never forget what you never knew. That made him think long and hard about Laia now. She been with him for three long years. Laia deserved at least an explanation. He decided to hear her out, even though it was not going to change his mind.

CHAPTER 6

"Here we go again, duh. Didn't you learn anything from the first time we met, Dante? I expect you to treat me like a lady and carry these bags for me. They are wearing down my shoulders and it is too heavy. So, are you taking me home or not? I told you that I quit. I'm going to have to leave the premises before the manager calls the police" cried Amar. She expected Dante to be her Knight in Shining Armor. She

Sparkle Riley

was not worrying about no girl in the car. Dante promised to do right by her, and she was holding him accountable to it.

"Here's what we're going to do. Write down your address and I will come by later tonight. I already made plans with my friends. Please understand Amar, but they did ask me first. I will pay for your cab home and I got a couple of dollars for you to order take out. But you are more than welcome to get dropped off by my friends. It is up to you. I am trying to work with you. And Amar as of now, I do not have a girlfriend. Kera and Tiana are just around the way girls. So, do not worry your pretty little head about it, kay" said Dante with a smile. Her lingo was wearing off on him big time. He made that comment intentionally to get a reaction out of her. It worked to perfection. Dang, I am the shit thought Dante Jones.

"Dante, those girlies in your car might be on you like that but trust and believe I'm not, kay. You are not even close to being my type. But I will take you up on your offer though. I will take the cab money. As soon as I get some money, I am going to pay you back every cent. I do not want you to be throwing it up in my face later, kay. And Dante do not expect none when you come over. Remember, me and you are not getting down like that. We, meaning you and I are just friends, kay" said Amar.

Dante was so mad at how she said what she said with such confidence. Anything was possible, she was not no Physic or Fortuneteller. Who do she think she is? Dante caught an instant attitude. Amar had a way of making him lose his cool. He was tired of Amar throwing it up in his face all the time that they were not a couple. It was like she was trying so hard not to like him. He was being a real gentleman to her and yet she barely acknowledged his efforts. Amar could not say that for her married Friend, Charles. Or whatever his name is? Amar failed to give him credit when it was clearly overdue. It angered him how Amar slept with Charles to get the damn job. She probably had to perform extra sexual favors for him to get it. Now she wants to up and quit like that. Charles should have given her car fare to get to and from work. That was the least that he could do. Deep down, he did not buy into Amar not wanting a man. Besides as of now, Amar was not even his girl and he was doing everything for her. He was about to even their score of exchanging words but decided not at this time.

"Oh, and here are your flying maxi-pads with wings. Don't wait up for me Bae" said Dante to be sarcastic. He would have stood there and talked for hours if Jermaine had not walked up to them. Jermaine was looking like a mad bull. Dante looked at his watch and realized that he had been rapping to Amar for about thirty minutes.

"Excuse Miss, I don't mean to interrupt. Dante, you do know that we been waiting in my hot car for a minute now. If it were not for everybody crying broke, I might could have turned my air on. Nobody got a dollar to put towards my gas" said Jermaine as he turned to sneak a glance at shorty in the

Sparkle Riley

nursing scrubs. He immediately extended his right hand to her and surprisingly she accepted his hand. Jermaine kissed her soft hands and took a bow. The fool even had the nerve to take off his Orioles hat for her. When Dante seemed to get bothered by it, Amar went all out. She daintily fluttered her big natural curly eyelashes at him. She started cooing and purring at him like a Persian Cat. Amar was batting her eyes and everything. She might as well, had crawled up on him and licked his face. Dante had to admit that it was very sultry and seductive performance on her part.

"I can see why my man kept you hidden beautiful. A splendid jewel, you are. My name is Jermaine Alston, and you are pretty lady?" said Jermaine. Amar was ready to turn out. What better way to get Dante's attention, she thought to herself? I will be going to the Strip Club after all. That is right I am going to start by screwing his homeboy when I get back from the Strip Club, too. Who does Dante Jones think

Sparkle Riley

he is? If he wants to play games then let the games begin, the voices in her head told her.

What a night they had! It was amazing how a little liquor does the body good. Time to turn up and get lit! The ladies really enjoyed themselves at Eldorado's Strip Club. Especially Miss. Amarylis Scott who came in first place for the amateur dance contest. Amar slid up and down that pole like a Goddess. She was flipping and doing splits. For the right cash, she was twerking butt naked. Tiana got on stage with her followed by Kera sliding up and down the pole. Dante and Jermaine were having the time of their lives. They all had a little too much to drink. Amar was loving all the love and attention. All eyes were fixated on her. Amar thought she was every man's fantasy and desire while up on stage. It was raining green dollars all around her. The sparkling glitter and confetti glistened all over her golden curves. Then she saw their faces in the audience. Her Ex Steven calling her a slut and a whore. Corey was slithering around her body like a snake. Winston was setting her body on fire. Ashtin was cutting her body up in pieces with a razor. Kyle her fiancé was trying to strangle her to death! The horrific hallucinations and the alcohol caused her to collapse on stage. Someone caught her in their arms and carried her off stage and into a car. That was all that Amar remembered as she continued to get sick on the car ride home.

So, since Jermaine's place was closer to the club, they decided to crash there for the night. The car ride seemed like an eternity! All she could feel was strong arms around her shoulders. Amar knew she was vomiting on that person's clothes too. He was wiping her face with a wet cool cloth. He kept her safe and warm. Whoever it was, held her hair away from her face. He held her hand so gently as he kissed it softly. Once at Jermaine's crib, the mystery man laid her on the sofa and covered her with blankets. They were all sprawled out all over the living room. Tiana made a bed on his kitchen table. Kera was curled up on the floor. Amar put her head under the blanket and that was it.

The next morning, the party gang woke up to the smell of fresh brewed coffee. Dante walked in on Kera and Tiana in the kitchen whispering to each other. When they saw Dante, they got quiet and the giggling stopped. It was a wild night of orgies and threesomes for some.

"Good morning beautiful ladies. Wasn't last night lit? Y'all was spoiling us brothers so nicely. Where's Amar and Jermaine at? Last night, we all crashed in here together. Amar was on the couch beside me, what happened?" said Dante. He heard them giggle on the low. Bold Tiana spoke first.

"I kept trying to give you some all night, Dante. If I am not mistaken, we both heard you say that you did not have no girl. You just straight flipped the script on me when Amarylis came around. Why is that?" said Tiana with a smirk on her face.

Sparkle Riley

"I'm still trying to figure out how you got any sleep. Neither of us could. Jermaine had Amarylis hollering all night after you went to sleep. I thought you and Amar were supposed to be talking or something? Because your homegirl was doing everything to him behind closed doors. Where you meet her at again? Was it her Only Fan's Page?' said Kera with a smile.

"You're right. I did say that because that is the truth ladies. We are not together. I guess she is a little freak then. She out here fucking any man breathing, huh. I am sorry about that Tiana. I did not mean to turn you down like that. I still had my ex on my mind. But if it is presented again, then I am down for whatever. Kera, I can take care of you too, Sweetie! Say Honey Dips, see if there is any whipped cream or peaches in Jermaine's fridge. I hope neither of you work this morning. Because I want to pay you and bless with my talented tongue and other big things" said Dante with a big revengeful smile. Dante feeling betrayed by Amar decided to get down and nasty with the two freaks. Now they would be even for now.

Amar rolled over to lay into Jermaine's arms. He was everything and more in bed. Now she could see herself cutting off all the other guys for him. Sike, she laughed to herself. But for real, Jermaine's lovemaking was superb! Pleasure was an understatement for a man with his master caliber. It felt good to not have to deny her sexual interests as a woman. That was the best part of being childless and single. You can be so liberated and free. Jermaine was the perfect antidote to clear her mind of Dante. He was getting too clingy and catching feelings. I did not come up here for all that thought Amar. Dante was getting too attached. She did not want to be loved or cared about like that. Dante was just doing too much! Amar was determined to put an end to it. Amar wanted to hurt him so bad. She smiled and rolled over on the other side to look at the clock on the dresser. "I wonder what time it is?" said Amar.

Sparkle Riley

"It's quarter to eleven Baby Girl" said a male voice beside her. It clearly was not Dante's sexy voice. That is when she realized what damage she really done. "Oh my God, I made a huge mistake" cried Amar as she buried her head under the soaked sweaty sheets. She burst into tears at the sight of their naked bodies entwined together.

"Jermaine, we really fucked up big time. I was so drunk and clearly not in my right mind. We can never tell anybody about this, Kay. Especially not Dante! I swear to God that I only wanted to pretend to have sex with you and that is on my Granny's grave" cried Amar.

"Shorty don't even sweat it. That little Thot Tiana was throwing it back at him all night. He was feeling down over his break-up with Laia, so I know he tapped that. Those two cousins are super freaks, so he probably fucked them both at the same time. We were all drunk and engaged in grown people sex. Besides Amarylis you came on to me first. It is all good, so just do not worry about it. Orgies is food for the

Sparkle Riley

soul! Trust me, because we all a bunch of freaks in this gang"
said Jermaine with a smirk. He was fantasizing about having
a group orgy in his mind. Amar saw his big erection through
his satin sheets. Amar looked over at him and he was
moaning and grabbing his wood with his eyes closed.
Seconds later, a big wet spot stained through his blue satin
sheets, again. Amar thought she heard a knock on the door.
She tried to shake Jermaine's arm, but he was in his zone.
After a few seconds, Jermaine came back to reality. When he
heard it, he jumped out of the bed fast and put his boxers
back on. He looked over at Amar in she was in tears again.
Jermaine walked over to her side of the bed to tell her to be
quiet.

"He will go away. But meanwhile pull yourself
together Amarylis. Who cares if Dante finds out about what
we did? He was out there getting his too. For the record, you
were not thinking about him for hours! Just keep your cool
and do not worry about him. Do you like him now or

Sparkle Riley

something? I do not want no bad blood between us. That is family right there. I advise you to just keep quiet about this" said Jermaine. He was started to panic now because he heard a knock on the door again. "Who is it?" yelled Jermaine.

"It's me Tiana. Y'all can come out now. There is no need to hide, so come on out. Your secret is safe with me. Dante is gone. Jermaine, me and Kera just need a ride home" said Tiana from outside the door. Amar was relieved and saved by the bell. Maybe he really did not know what happened between them, she thought.

"Amar, you get dressed too. I am not driving back and forth in all this heat. If you need a ride, you better be ready on this go round. Ain't none of y'all got gas money. I had a good time shorty, but you gots to go" said Jermaine. He told Tiana that he would be right out to take them home. Amar did as she was told and got dressed. Now the grease was about to hit the fan for sure, she thought. She just wanted to go home and take a long hot shower.

Amarylis had Dante on her mind something fierce. It was her second night in Baltimore City. It was already a disaster. Everything was spiraling out of control. Why she even cared about Dante's feeling were scaring her to death. It was not supposed to be like that. This was not in her plan at all. Dante should have left her standing with her bags on her shoulder. Now they got a problem on deck. Dante was blocking her game big time. If he had never showed his feelings for her, none of this would have happened. The whole car ride was silent. Kera was sitting up front looking out the window. Tiana was sitting in the back seat looking sad and stupid

Dante had already told her to keep what they did between them. He did not want Amar to find out about them. Tiana and Kera was confused because he claimed that he and Amar were not an item. They do not even talk or mess around like that. Yet, he wanted to keep it a secret from her. Kera did not really care to much for Dante, but Tiana did.

After everything he did to her, she thought that he liked her like that. When they got done, Dante told her they are never hooking up again and to not contact him again. Tiana felt so used and irrelevant. She did not even want to look at Amarylis because her feelings got hurt. Amar was a freak just like her and she still had Dante on her. It was just not fair, thought Tiana.

Amar was starting to remember bits and pieces about the party. She remembered seeing Tiana kissing all over him. Dante was smiling at her while he was feeling her up. Dante looked her right in the eye as he put a hickey on Tiana's neck. Amar knew he was mad because she went to a motel with Charles. It was crazy because they had an understanding or at least that was what she thought.

Jermaine pulled up to Monument and Preston Street to drop off Amar. He had an attitude with her the whole car ride. He saw Amarylis as a threat between him and Dante.

Sparkle Riley

It was obvious that his homeboy had some type of feelings for her. Jermaine knew he should have turned it down because Amar was drunk. But by being a single man, he just could not resist Amar's advances. Besides, Dante was not claiming her. What was he supposed to do in that situation? He parked his car in front of the house and let Amar out. No one said goodbye or see you later. Amar just threw her bags over her shoulders and kept it moving. She did not look back either. It was just a one-time thing. They were not her friends and Jermaine was not her man. It was just sex with him and nothing more.

Amar was about to put her key to unlock the door. It was amazing how bad things just kept happening to her. She was always caught up in some mess with somebody. Her life was getting complicated. She made it her business not to get caught up over no guy and here she goes again. She did not leave Georgetown, South Carolina to get caught up in some

Sparkle Riley

Baltimore City Shit! As soon as she opened the door, her heart skipped a beat.

"What took you so long Amar? Look we need to talk for real. I am not your man and I get that. You can do you and it is none of my business Amar. But I lost my little sister to these streets and I am not trying to lose you like that too. This trashy room ain't no place for a girl like you. You are too out there. Your risky and promiscuous behavior is going to get you hurt or killed. Living in a big city all alone like this is too dangerous. My mama got an extra room at her place. I mentioned that before and you just brushed it off. But for real Amar, you need to reconsider. It is for you, not me. Just keep those bags on your shoulders because we are out of here. I talked to your Landlord and it is all good in the hood. I won't take no for an answer so we out!" said Dante. He was surprised that Amar agreed this time. He did not know what that was about. They both left and were standing on the corner trying to flag down a hack. Amar had this guilty look

Sparkle Riley

on her face and so did he. He kept having flashbacks about Tiana and Kera! Dante had his bags on his shoulders too. He had his head down so low that he bumped right into somebody walking past him. All he could see was himself on his knees naked with whipped cream all over his mouth. Tiana had squeezed her legs around his neck. When he got done, he stood up. Tiana stood up and blocked him by pressing her body up against him seductively.

"Going so soon, Dante. So, do we talk now or are we dating now? I did not want this to be a one-night stand. Look we're both single, so what's up?" said Tiana.

Dante did not have time for Tiana. It was just mind-blowing sex, no more and no less. He had no intentions of making Tiana or anybody else his girl. He had to close the door with Laia first. But right now, he was heading straight toward Amar. Tiana started crying and everything.

"Tiana, I ain't sign up to be your man. It ain't even like that. We cool, but that is just about it. We did what we did

Sparkle Riley

and that is it. It was good. I cannot lie about that. I just advise

you not to speak about it to anyone. I know you feel salty

towards Amar, but I am warning you to keep your mouth

closed. I am not for your games Tiana. Just let it go, kay.

You got what you always wanted from me. I laid down the

pipe on it and I am out" said Dante and he pushed past her.

Tiana stepped aside to let him pass by with an attitude. That

was her problem not his, thought Dante. A hack in a silver

Nissan Sentra stopped to pick them up on Monument Street.

This time he asked Amar to let him please carry the bags on

her shoulder. He was getting the hang of it slowly but surely.

The car ride was awkward and quiet. The only time that he

spoke was to tell the guy to go to 5604 Sinclair Lane and that

he only had twelve dollars to his name

The eighteen- minute ride to his mama's crib had his

thoughts twisted in circles. Amarylis Scott was changing his

life. He could hit himself in the head for getting himself

caught up again. Why didn't I just leave her on the corner

with her bags? He just had to stop and stare at a pretty face. The bad part was that they could never be. Neither of them wanted to be together like that. With her bags on his shoulders, Dante used the key to open the door. He stepped to the side to let Amar in first. She was happy and smiling to his surprise.

"Amar, please make yourself at home. My mom sis at work. She will be back by dinner. You hungry? I can fix us something to eat. I got a little skills in the kitchen. You can have my bedroom and I will take the basement. My sister's room is off limits. We left the room the way she left it. You got any questions for me?" said Dante. Amar was ready to go off up in there!

"Dante, have you lost your mind? I got a problem with this here living arrangements! You expect me to live with your mama now. I do not know that lady like that. Shoot, I do not even like you like that for real. And you going to be staying here too. What is this Dante? You and me are not an

Sparkle Riley

item. We discussed that already! Are you doing all this to screw me? Or are you trying to take advantage of me, huh? Like I told you before I am not nobody's wifey. You are going to expect me to cook and clean for you and shit. Make me wash and iron your dirty stinking clothes! You not getting no free in house coochie either. I am not laying on my back for you at the drop of a dime. Meanwhile, you will be out here screwing everything in a skirt. Hell, to the no Dante, kay! This shit is not going to work Partner! You got to do better than this right here Dante" said Amar with an attitude. Dante loved a lady with a little fire in her. That little bossy chick right there did it for him too. Miss. Peachy Sunshine was hard to please and he admired that. Amar spoke her mind and liked to be in control of things. "South Carolina is in the house" said Dante under his breath. He could not stop smiling because Amar did not have the Southern Charm that he expected.

"Fool, what in the hell is so funny, huh? What are you geeking for? I am like at the bottom of a barrel, so you got one on me. Just this one- time though. I am not trying to make this no habit. I cannot front because I have nowhere else to go. I know you been plotting this here since the day you met me. But I cannot blame you. Look at me, I got you tripping over me. Don't lie, you like me don't you Dante Jones?" said Amar.

"Only in your dreams Amar. I do not have to stay here with you, kay. I got plenty of chicks who would gladly take in and treat me like a king. I told you I had a sister and I know these streets Amar. I do not have nothing up my sleeve. You have my word on that. I just wanted to be a nice guy to you. I felt sorry for you and I wanted to help" said Dante sympathetically. Amar went into an unexpected rage. Dante said the wrong words at the wrong time!

Amar started to throw chairs at him. She knocked everything off the dining room table. Fine china and stained

Sparkle Riley

glasses were cracked all over the floor. His mama's chairs were broken into pieces. Amar was having another meltdown. She started crying and everything. Dante went over and gave her a hug. He kissed her softly on the forehead with tears in his eyes

"Amarylis I am deeply sorry for what I said. It was very inconsiderate of me to make you feel like a charity case. Please let me be the friend that helps you. I will never hurt you or take advantage of you because you are a woman. I want to be that shoulder to cry on. Let me carry the bags on your shoulders for a change. Do not worry, I got you Amar. I know you hate all men right now and I get that. But you can let your guard down around me. You will be safe here with us. My Mama Siarra is going to love you too. Oops, did I say that out loud. But anyway, I think you get what I am saying. Just let me clean this mess up first and then I will draw you a warm bubble bath. I do massages and everything Girl. If you did not know, you better ask somebody" said Dante Jones.

"I have no words left Dante. You are not kicking me out or nothing. Who are you Dontae and what planet did you come from? To this day, you have not pressured me to have sex with you or anything. I always wanted to be treated like a princess you know. Today, I can admit that I do not deserve to be put on a pedestal at all. Dante, I am not that person that you want me to be though. I am a bad and vengeful person Dante. I am selfish too. I only love Amarylis and I do not give a damn about anyone else. I will use you Dante until your water runs dry. I got to many problems and issues. I have a hard time accepting the hand that I was dealt. I have a habit of blaming others for my mistakes while not taking accountability for my part in it. I ain't no good for you" cried Amar.

"Amarylis nobody is perfect. Then use and abuse me. Get that shit over with and out of your system. I get where you are coming from? I understand completely and I can deal with it. Nothing that you say or do will ever change that. You are right for me and at the right time in my life. Look at me, do I look perfect to you? I have my flaws too. If this is about you and Jermaine, Sweetie I know. It was my fault really. I led you to him. I tried to put Tiana all up in your face. You said that you did not want me over and over. I lost control for a minute. Check this out. I ain't no saint either. I slept with Tiana and her cousin when I found out about you and Jermaine. I know that was childish, but I had to get even with you Amar. I apologize for that" said Dante. He walked over again to try to kiss her on the lips this time. But Amar pushed him back. She put the palms of her hand up to his face instead. She was not trying to go there yet with Dante.

"Don't! Dante, if you want to draw me a bath, that is fine. I will even let you give me a massage. But that is it, kay! So, what we are even. That does not change anything in my book. I messed up your mama's house, so it is only right that I help clean it up to. This is a hell of a way to make a first impression, right? I think it is better for you and I to just

Sparkle Riley

be friends. You are out here screwing around and so am I. Being in a love triangle ain't cool, you know. I need to get myself together. I came all the way from South Carolina a hot mess. I need a job and a place of my own before I can even think of you like that. We need to get this cleaned up before Ms. Siarra comes home" said Amar. Dante felt rejected and used again. If a friend is what she wanted, then that is what she will get, thought Dante. It was obvious that Amar had hoe tendencies. So now it was on. He decided that he was not going to sit around and wait on her no more. They are both single, just living under the same roof.

"I am going to order us carryout if that is ok. I will introduce you to my moms and all that good stuff. You know, get you acquainted and situated. Then I got to step out for a minute. Everything is going to work out for you here. You are safe, kay. If you ever need someone to talk to, I will be here for you, always" said Dante.

Sparkle Riley

They both cleaned up the mess on the floor together.

Neither of them said a word. Afterwards, he ran her bath as

promised. He cancelled the nude hot oil massage and Amar

understood why. About an hour later, their carryout arrived.

They even sat in the kitchen and ate in silence, too. Dante

removed the two white foam cartons from the plastic bags.

Amar's eyes lit up over Dante's hook up. She had packs of

hot sauce, salt and pepper. The crispy fried chicken was

smothered in butter sauce, season salt and Old Bay. The

western fries were drowning in pools of ketchup. The buttery

sweet cornbread had her over the moon. Amar was ready to

dive in. Dante was still in his feelings while trying to enjoy

his meal with her

"A thank-you would be nice. Money does not grow on

trees you know. I got a lot of things to figure out today" said

Dante as he opened his chicken box. He used his teeth to

open his hot sauce packs. He was clearly giving her mad

Sparkle Riley

attitude. Amar decided not to feed into it though. Amar was smacking on her chicken when she said the unthinkable.

"Something on your mind Partner. I got a few minutes now. I ain't going to beg you to tell me. I got problems myself. I swore down that I would never live with a dude again and here I go. Believe me, you are my last resort. We will be sharing the same space and everything now. I don't even know you like that" said Amar. Now that was the final straw for Dante. He had been keeping everything boiling inside. Now the kettle pot had tipped off the stove. He lashed out at her in rage.

"You know I don't get you Amarylis Scott. You are always so hard on me. You are out here screwing all these random dudes with no questions asked. But you expect me to do everything for you though. Where's Jermaine or Charles at? I got your back more than they do. I never asked for anything in return. You want me to be near and far away too. Well Amar, you cannot have your cake and eat it too. This

Sparkle Riley

has nothing to do with you screwing my homeboy either.
You come in my life with bags on your shoulders and cause
me nothing but problems. I got a car and a place already. I
got my ex texting me to death and yet I am here with you! I
was supposed to be putting in a 60-day notice. Laia still has
my car. I know that she cannot keep up with the payments
and car insurance. After three years, I'm out" said Dante with
an attitude.

CHAPTER 7

"Oh Lordt, I can't believe that I got another cry baby
on my hands. Dante why are you sitting here telling me all
this for? Am I supposed to be jealous or something? That is
the thing that I do not like about you. You do not have a
backbone. You let your ex run all over the top of you. Instead
you sit here and whine to your crush. I get it, you are
infatuated with me. Trust me, that is all it is. I am different
from the types of girls that you are used to. For the record, I

Sparkle Riley

never met a guy like you before either. But that does mean that we should be a couple Dante. What is Ms. Siarra going to say about all of this, huh? I have to get in your mama's good graces. If I am not your love interest, she may not want me to stay. What if you and Laia get back together? I might decide to kick it with Jermaine from time to time. Our friendship will be ruined before it even has the chance to blossom Dante" said Amar. I am the third wheel again. Dante, Dante, I should have just walked away. Dante was just on a break from his girl, thought Amar I could not resist him. Now this is the price that I pay. Unbelievably, she was playing herself again.

"No this can work. You and I are just going to have rules and regulations. I do not get you women sometimes. Just because I am not disrespectful and dogging you out, I am weak, huh. You would not be saying that if I was cussing you out or putting my hands on you though. At the end of the day Amar, this is just a temporary arrangement anyway. I am

Sparkle Riley

going to my basement bedroom if you care to know" said

Dante as he walked away from her.

Amar was tied. After eating and arguing, she went

upstairs to Dante's room. She was amazed at how neat and

clean it was. She looked in his closets and saw that he ironed

his clothes. He had them on hangers too. Amar was

impressed like a pig in mud. He had his tennis shoes in their

original boxes. There was a picture of Laia on his dresser.

Amar was curious and nosey, so she opened the top drawer.

She saw something in there that shed a new light on Dante

Jones.

Siarra Jones walked into the delicious aroma of

seasoned Pork Chops and BBQ Spareribs. She thought she

had entered a twilight zone. "Dante boy, what are you up to

now? What did you do now? I am not paying no bail or no

traffic tickets" she said. Dante snuck up from behind her and

gave her a big hug.

Sparkle Riley

"Ma, why do I have to be in some sort of trouble, huh? I cannot cook a nice dinner for my own mama and a friend. I will not beat around the bush about it because I know that you are not for no games. Mama, I brought a friend here to stay with us. Here me out before you cuss me out, kay. Her name is Amarylis Scott from South Carolina. I met her at the bus stop with just the bags on her shoulders the other day. We been cool like that since that day. Ma, she does not have anywhere else to go. She does not have any family or friends either. She was renting a room over on Monument and Preston. So, you know where I am coming from right? It is only temporary kay. I want to help her get on her feet and that is it. No need to take off your belt or hit me with the fly smacker" said Dante with a smile. He went on to tell his mama that she was upstairs sleeping. He told her about Amar's tragic past. His mama was totally on board with it and understood completely.

Sparkle Riley

"Son, you always had a heart of gold. I know that this has a lot to do with your sister's death. I know that you blame yourself for it, Dante. But it was nobody's fault but her own. She was a young adult that made bad decisions. She fell in with a bad group of girls, drugs and boys. We did everything in our power to save her and she knows that too. Even for Miss. Scott, there is only but so much that you can do for her. I will do my part to help her too. Just please do not get yourself caught up with this chick from out of town. I already lost your sister and I will be damned if I lose you to the streets, too. Well what are you waiting for Dante? Tell Amarylis to come down to dinner. I can't wait to meet the girl that caught your eye" said Siarra.

Amar came downstairs to find Ms. Siarra sitting on the sofa. Dante looked exactly like his mama. She had the same gray cat eyes too. She was very stunning. Miss. Siarra had her in purple Faux locks and stood at about as tall as Dante.

"You must be Amarylis. Please come take a seat beside me. I have heard so much about you Miss. South Carolina, come" said Siarra as she patted to the seat beside her. Amar was loving her charming poise and demeanor already. Now she knew where Dante's good traits came from. Her home felt warm and inviting. It reminded her of Grandma Estelle's Cottage back home.

"Ms. Jones, I really appreciate everything that you and Dante are doing for me. You opened your home to me like I am family. Trust me, I do not deserve all of this. I was a loving and caring person years ago and I am not that sweet person anymore. I just cannot be good, no matter how hard I try. Dante is a fine young man and I would never intentionally set out to hurt him. But I cannot always control my behavior if that makes any sense. I will not let him get caught up with me because I do care about him a lot. I will never tell him that though" said Amar.

"Young lady, you are very impressive indeed. I can see why my son is so fond of you. You are so up front and direct. I like you already. Just to let you know Amarylis, I am going to help you too. Here, take a hug dear" said Siarra. She reached over and squeezed Amarylis real tight. Amar reciprocated back with the same intense hug. The two ladies were enjoying their conversations together while Dante was in the kitchen preparing a scrumptious dinner.

Dante had on his apron and was throwing down in the kitchen, while Amar sat in the living room with his mother. At times Amar was happy while other times she felt inadequate and lost. It felt so awkward at times because she was often at a loss for words. Ms. Jones was nice and all but still it was his mama. Ms. Jones kept looking in her face, at her shoes and at her trembling hands.

"You're nervous Miss. Scott. That is how I was when I met Dante's father's mother. A year later we were married. God rest his soul, he died tragically when Dante and Tashay

Sparkle Riley

were little. He was my everything Girl. When he died, a part of me died too. I became a single mama and I did what I had to do to survive. It was not easy, but I made it through. Then we lost Tashay. Enough about me, I want to get to know my baby boy's new girlfriend. He hasn't brought any of them to the house before" said Ms. Jones.

Oh child, thought Amar. It is about to get hot and heavy. Her hands got all warm, moist and tingly. She hated Dante Jones now more than ever. He was trying to pull her leg. Who did he think he was, she thought to herself? Every time she is around him, it is always some sort of problem.

"Ms. Jones, I thought I explained our relationship to you. I do not want to be rude, but I was very up front with you about us. I do not want to hurt your son or string him along. One day he will be the perfect Prince Charming to the right lady. One day, I hope to turn my duffle bags into to just one sparkling diamond clutch purse. I did not make him do any of this, I swear to you. He is doing all of this out of the

Sparkle Riley

kindness of his heart. Dante and I are just going to be roommates. I came up from South Carolina to start a new chapter in my life. I met your son and now I am here. I was renting a room on Monument Street, but that did not work out. Dante had just broke-up with his girlfriend and moved out when we met. We will have to go out and look for a place together. I have to get a Maryland ID and everything first. Dante is a big help" said Amar while blushing. Siarra's whole mood changed after that. She now saw Amarylis as an opportunist who would stop at nothing to get what she wants.

"Are you ladies in here talking about me behind my back? You know that I am the Chef, right? I got some Pork Chops smothered in green peppers and onions. I prepared my world- famous BBQ ribs for this occasion too. I whipped up homemade mashed potatoes and cream of corn, just for my two favorite ladies" said Dante with a smile. He was full of jokes, thought Amar. Cooking an intimate dinner for the three of them was too much. Amar wondered what happened between him and Laia? He seemed like an ok dude to her.

Ms. Jones knew what was up. Her son obviously had a thing for Miss. Scott and the feeling was mutual to a certain extent. Amarylis would gladly be taking advantage of her Dante if he let her. She also found it hard to believe that he had broken up with Laia. The two of them have been going back and forth for years. For him to bring in another woman was new to her. Amar seemed nice. It was easy to see her pain. It was in the way that she talked. Ms. Jones could tell that she had been through a lot. She just hoped that the young lady was not in over her head. Dante will always go back to Laia! Amar was just smiling and smiling and surprisingly so was he.

"Only good things Son. This is a marvelous dinner that you cooked up. You have only cooked like this for your family once! No offense, Miss. Scott. After dinner, we will all need to sit down and talk this through. I hear that you two

Sparkle Riley

are moving in together Dante" said Ms. Scott. Amar had a nervous look on her face, while Dante was happy and confident. Whew, what a relief thought Amar. Amar had not mentioned that to Dante yet!

"Um, I was thinking about it before I took my nap Dante. I thought that maybe you and I could get a place together for at least a year. We both will be able to save up our money to go separate ways. We are already roommates now. So, I do not see what the difference would be" said Amar. Siarra started frowning up in disgust!

"Amar, you and I can discuss that in private, kay. Let us all just eat and enjoy this dinner that I prepared all by myself" said Dante. He could cut the tension in the air with a knife. The ladies shook their heads in agreement. Dante blessed their food, and everyone devoured the food that was on their plates. Dinner with Dante and his mom was alright, thought Amar. The fake and light conversations were anything but refreshing. It was dull and stale, like forced air.

Sparkle Riley

Dante was charming and entertaining with a touch of Southern Charm. But during dessert, things got a little more tense. Ms. Jones whole demeanor had changed from pleasant to serious.

"Ma, I surprised you, didn't I? I even took off my bandana and pulled my jeans up. I know you both like my diamond belt. Please Do not jump up all at once. Ma, what is wrong now? I am going to clean up the kitchen and do the dishes. I just wanted to do something nice for a change. What did I do?" said Dante.

"Oh no Son, everything was perfect. I got to meet your new friend. You did a superb job with our dinner and dessert. I loved it! I just have reservations about your moving in together. You two hardly know each other Dante. I did not even know that you and Laia had broken up for the 100th time. I would like to offer our home to Amarylis until she gets herself together. If that is ok with the two of you. I can even help her find a job and a place of her own. I can do that

Sparkle Riley

better than you can Honey. I just do not want the two of you living together" said Ms. Jones.

Amar looked hurt and surprised. She thought everything was going good between them. Dante was good for her. She did not care about his ex. They were going to sign a lease together so the hell with Laia. Besides, it was his choice and not Ms. Siarra's. As far as she knew he had not been in contact with her since the break-up. So, she totally disagreed with his mother. It was nice of her to offer her hospitality, but it was not going down like that. Her and Dante was moving in together no matter what she said.

"Ma, why do you have to bring Laia into this. It is really over this time. Is this about what she posted on Facebook, Ma? Laia is not pregnant and I know that for a fact. Why do I have to stay with her if I do not want to Ma? She is not the only woman in the world. Why can't I have lady friends, huh? Dad had lots of female friends and you were ok with that!" said Dante.

Sparkle Riley

"Yeah, but in the end, he broke her heart. Your dad led her on to believe that she had a chance. Brittany had fallen head over hills for your dad. I am not implying that this is the case for you two. I just think the two of you shouldn't rush into anything" said Ms. Jones.

"With all due respect Mam, I totally disagree. Dante is a grown man. As for me, I am not out here looking for love. I have been there and done that several times. I got stood up at my own wedding not too long ago. So, I think I know what I am doing. I am not going to stop him from going back to Laia, if that is what he chooses to do. That would be his choice to make. I appreciate your kind gesture from the heart, but I will have to turn you down respectively" said Amar.

Ms. Jones had no choice but to let it go for now. She did not want to ruin her son's dinner over Amar's selfishness. Amar was very outspoken and strong willed. She was the type that wants what she wants and that was that. She obviously had her eyes and pockets set on snagging Dante by

Sparkle Riley

any means necessary. Woman to woman, Amarylis would just have to find out the hard way then, thought Ms. Jones. A mother always knows the intentions of her only son.

"You're right Honey. As an adult, you should make your own decisions. Just make sure they are yours and that you are not being influenced by others. As a man, you still need to reach out to Laia regarding her possible pregnancy. Even if she is not pregnant Dante, she still deserves closure" said Ms. Jones. Dante was already planning on seeing her later anyway.

Her comes the shade and the attitude. Amar was going in for the kill on that remark. Once again, her personal experiences from the past were spiking through the present. She just could not leave the past behind her. Amar stood up at the table with her hands on her hips!

"Dante does not owe her a damn thing, Ms. Jones! No man has ever given me closure and I had to deal with it. My own mother left me on my Granny's front porch. I was a little girl. Years later, my Granny committed suicide. I did

not get a goodbye note. I did not find out why until years

later. If I had to go through it, so can Laia!" yelled Amar.

"I'm sorry that it happened that way. That was your

painful experience Love. How can you stand there and wish

it on another woman like that? You cannot just go around

blaming everybody for the bad hand that you were dealt. The

world does not owe you anything, your mama does! You stay

running with your bags. It is about time that you accept what

has happened to you Miss. Scott. I will not allow you to use

Dante as your personal crutch. I know that your torn and

fragile, so I will excuse this evenings outburst. But I had

better not see it happen again, kay. That tough exterior does

not intimidate me Boo. If you want to live under my roof,

you will respect me and Dante! Do I make myself perfectly

clear young lady? Because if you don't you will be throwing

them bags right back over your shoulders again!" said Siarra.

Sparkle Riley

"Yes Mam, Ms. Siarra. You have the upper hand for right now. If you both could please excuse me, I would like to resort to my room please" said Amar as she stomped up the steps to Dante's bedroom. "That bitch just got on my shit list. Siarra think that she is going to talk to me any kind of way. Just because I am at a disadvantage does not give her the right to talk to me like trash. Siarra ain't my damn mama. I swear she will regret roasting me in front of my meal ticket" said Amar under her breath. Oh, it was on and popping now. South Carolina is in your house!

Later that evening, Dante visited Laia. They made up and made love.

CHAPTER 8

Dante could not believe that a whole month had gone by. He was smiling as he opened the mailbox. Amar's Maryland ID Card came in the mail. He ran upstairs and knocked on her door to give her the good news. He had to knock real hard because Amar had the radio music blasting.

Sparkle Riley

"Jermaine, get off me now! Dante's nuisance ass is at my door again. You are going to have to go out of the window again. Before, you go I am going to need a couple of dollars. You been laying up under me for a month now!" yelled Amar.

"I just gave you three-hundred dollars the other day. Dang Girl, you spent that up already. I still got to pay for your traffic tickets. I keep telling you to stop speeding and running red lights in my car Amar. It seems like your trying to take advantage of me a little. You got me sneaking in and out of my homeboy's windows and shit. This is not working for me no more Amar. I am going to give you this cash but after that, I am through with you. You are going to have to find another sucker to suck dry. Here take this shit and loose my digits!" said Jermaine. He hurried and put his clothes and jumped out of the first- floor window for the last time. Jermaine was glad to get rid of her country behind. Amar smiled as he jumped out the window. It did not matter to her

Sparkle Riley

if he came back or not. She already got everything that she wanted from him. Amar walked over to let Dante in his bedroom.

"Amar, Girl open up a window in here. It smells musty in here. Look, your ID came today. So now I can take you out to fill out job applications. Get dressed, today is going to be a good day, kay" said Dante with a smile. Amar put up her middle finger to him.

"Dante, I been texting you all day. Where you been, huh? We are supposed to be roommates. We are not spending time in any of the rooms in this house. I want you to know that I don't appreciate that at all" said Amar. Dante did not want to have that conversation with her again. That is why he had been avoiding her lately. He also knew that she was not going to let him off the hook that easily. His mama was sick of her that she hardly stayed at home. Most of the time, she spent the night over her new friend's house.

"That is the thing Amar. You and I are roommates and we both agreed on it. I am busy during the day. You said that you been texting me all day. Is there something that you need Amar? You have your own toiletries and laundry detergent. What else do you need?" said Dante.

"Oh, that is how it is now. You just going to leave me holed up in this house all day by myself. Have you forgotten everything that I been through Dante? I am the victim here. Look at me when I am talking to you Dante. It is Ms. Siarra, isn't it? She is still badmouthing me to you. What do you want me to do all day? I do not have anyone to talk to, hello!" yelled Amar. Dante hated when she put the guilt trip on him every time. It was true, he still had a soft spot for her. But it was more a sisterly love now. He and Laia were going real strong again. Laia got rid of the dog and she had a little job now. She was contributing to the bills now. Life was good. He was just waiting for the right time to tell Amar. He was tired of spending the night at both places because

Sparkle Riley

technically he was supposed to be at his own place with his girl. Amar was getting big and lazy now.

"Look, I wasn't going to say anything because it is none of my business. But my boy across the street been peeping you out. He said that you be having different men running in and out of my mother's house. You be driving their cars around town, so why are you so bored?" said Dante. Amar was ready to throw the book at him. Dante had the audacity to stand there and act all innocent.

"Ok, you got one on me. But look here Partner, I be peeping you too. I be seeing you and Laia riding around town too. I did not know you two were back together. You never said anything to me about it. And you know of my traumatic past regarding being left in the dark. I thought you were putting in a 60-day notice. Did you or not? The last time that we talked, you and I were getting a place together. Did that change too? I am easy to get along with Dante. Just do not play with my intelligence, kay. You were the one that brought me here and you better not forget that. I was fine where I was staying. Can you at least help me get a Driver's license then?" said Amar. Dante agreed because he felt guilty once again. He was also happy that she was taking the news about Laia and him so well. So, he figured that was the least that he could do.

Amar intentionally kept him out all day. By the time they got back, it was too late to go home to Laia. When they walked up the driveway, Dante noticed an unfamiliar car there.

"Looks like, your mama has got company too. You know you never told me that you had a little Toyota Dante. You really surprised me with that one" said Amar. She was getting tied of Dante keeping secrets from here. This one was the icing on the cake. After everything that she confided in him. Dante still was doing her dirty on purpose.

"Jermaine knew somebody that was selling it for cheap. Most of the time, I have it parked over at Laia's place.

It makes my insurance cheaper having two cars. It is really good on gas too" said Dante.

Amar decided to add her Southern Charm to the mix. It had worked on all the other guys, so it would be just as easy to use it on Dante. She saw an opportunity to decided to shoot her shot at him. All she had to do with him is lay a guilt trip on him. She also had to pretend to respect and support he and Laia's relationship. Amar did not give a damn about it but that was not the point. Dante had something that she needed. With Jermaine out of the picture she needed some wheels to get from point A to point B and Dante was just the sucker to do it. Dang, I am the that boss chick, thought Amar to herself.

They walked in and ran right into her mama's new boyfriend. Dante had met him once, but Amar had not. Amar thought that was real disrespectful because she was a part of the family too. Amar hated being treated like she was invisible all the time. Miss. Siarra came into the living room

Sparkle Riley

as soon as they came in. Her new eye candy was looking all in her face like she was a snack. Amar already knew what time it was by the man winking his eye at her.

"Dante, you remember Ricky. He was just leaving" said Siarra. She acted like did she did not see her standing there. Amar did not care about Siarra being ignorant because her man sure was checking her out in the corner of his eye.

"Ms. Siarra, hello! I am here too. Excuse me Sir, my name is Amarylis Scott and yours please?" said Amar as she batted her eyelashes. That worked like a charm every time. Amar intentionally rubbed her booty against him as she squeezed by. Dante was grateful that his mama did not catch her doing that mess. Even he was mesmerized by that big thing attached toa tiny waist. Ricky was so embarrassed that he ran out of there quick. He barely said goodbye to his mama. Dante decided not to bring it up. He decided to just brush it off. He knew that Amar was not that crazy to mess

Sparkle Riley

around with his mama's new boyfriend. So, he simply let it go.

After a long day, all he wanted to do was to go in the basement and sleep. That would be after he explained the situation to Laia. They were really in a good place now. Laia trusted him more and was not as insecure as before. They did not keep any secrets between them. Laia knew all about his Homegirl Amar. At least, most of it. Too much would risk their relationship to go backwards again.

Amar got up to go to the bathroom and ran right into Siarra. His mama stood there mugging her and everything. She obviously had something steam that she wanted to let off. So, Amar propositioned her to speak her peace.

"Amarylis, there are two things that I do not play around with. One is my money and two is my man. Now woman to woman. I am going to let this be your one and only verbal warning. You have been here a month now and still do not have your shit together young lady. But now we got a

Sparkle Riley

problem Dear. I do not want any other woman around my man. I should not have to stay over at his house because you are in mines. My man should be welcome to spend the night in my house freely. I saw the way that you were looking at him Amar. I think all of Baltimore City knows that you are a little country whore by now. Your name always come up in the Nail Salons and Barber Shops. Personally, I do not care what STD you catch. Just do not pass it on to my son or his long-term girlfriend, kay" said Siarra. Amar was not even going to feed into that bull. She was going to feed her man instead. Ms. Siarra was wrong for trying to take it there for real. That was totally uncalled for and unnecessary. But if that is how she feels, so be it! Amar was tired of everybody turning their noses down on her because she had issues.

"Ms. Siarra, I will not stoop to your level because you are old enough to be my mama. I do not have time for this. I just want to do what I got do and then roll out. My friendship with Dante is too important to me. I got up to use the bathroom and that is it. You have a good night now. See you bright and early in the morning, kay" said Amar and brushed past her.

Amar had to hurry to get back to her room because Charles was coming through again. Poor Charles really got himself caught up bad, thought Amar. He was behind on his mortgage, child support payments and student loans messing with her behind. He was steps away from getting his car repossessed too. Charles was becoming a nuisance. He was always whining and crying broke. Amar decided it was time to kick him to the curb because he was of no more use to her. When he came through her window it was on! "Charles, Dexter or whatever your name is? Climb your tall behind right back out!" said Amar.

Amar woke up to the smell of bacon, grits, toast and ham. She figured that Dante must be throwing down in the kitchen again. Ms. Siarra's insecure behind was at work. Amar was walking down the hallway when she noticed that

Siarra's bedroom door was open. Since they had a fallout the previous night before it made her want to be nosey. Amar noticed that her purse was open and on her bed. She went straight for Siarra's wallet. Amar made it her business to clean it out. It was a hundred dollars inside of it and she stole sixty of it. Amar put it back exactly the way that she found it. She stuffed the bills in her bra and rolled out. Amar smiled because she had got back at Siarra for disrespecting her. This was just the beginning of their drama.

Dante was standing at the stove scrambling eggs when Amar walked into the kitchen. He fresh oranges and bananas swirling in a blender. English muffins had popped out of the toaster. Dante was in a bright sunny mood. He was all smiles when he saw Amar. She was still the apple of his eye. He started blushing as soon as she started smiling. Dante immediately ran over to pull out the chair for her. Amar was blushing as she sat down. Dante still had it as far as she was concerned.

Sparkle Riley

"Good morning Sunshine! I just thought I would cook up a little something something. Let me fix your plate Miss. Scott. I have fresh peaches and strawberries too!" said Dante. Now Amar would tell anybody that she has been around the block. She had seen and done it all. Amar knew that a man was that happy, he normally had bad news to tell. Dante spent the whole day with her yesterday and now he surprised her with breakfast. Amar knew for a fact that Laia would not be ok with that. It must be trouble in paradise. Thought Amar. She let him put on his charade and even played along with him. They had a delicious, romantic breakfast together. Dante told jokes and showered her with compliments. Amar had enough and stood up with her hands on her hips. Dante was going overboard with her hair compliments and that was pissing her off.

"Look I appreciate our little breakfast with refreshing conversations. But when you kept telling me my hair looks beautiful, you got on my poop list. I am to mad to say the shit word right now. Lay it on me Dante. Tell me the bad news. I am tough and I can handle anything. I cannot say that I did not see this coming. In fact, I should have expected this from you. You are leaving me, aren't you? Do not lie about it, Dante. You are no different from all the rest of the guys!" said Amar. Dante could not believe that she hit it right on the nose. Amar must be psychic, thought Dante.

"You are right Amar, but it is not what you think. I can never leave you because we will always be friends. But I am leaving town though. Laia wants us to move to New York to be with her family. Her dad owns a restaurant there and he is going to hook me up with a gig. And get this, he has an apartment right above it. Laia and I will living there rent free. We just have to work in the restaurant. I am so excited. Aren't you happy for me Amar?' said Dante.

"Fool, are you crazy? I can see packing your bags to run away from a problem. But you are packing right into one. You need to run in the opposite direction as fast as you can.

Sparkle Riley

Once you get around her family, Laia is going to go back to her old ways again. She is going to make you her slave. Being bossy and demanding would be an understatement. Besides, you are a poet. Why would you want to wash dishes and wait tables for free?" said Amar. Dante was furious as he paced the kitchen floor.

"Wait, how did you know that Amar? Have you been snooping through my things? You had no business doing that behind my back. I invite you and let you stay here for free and you cannot respect my things. Do you know how many times my mama wanted to kick you out on the street Amar? I did that for you. I gave my mom's an ultimatum for you. I always had your back no matter what. Either we both stay, or I am leaving with you. I sacrificed everything for you girl. I have always been your Knight in Shining Armor. I treated you like my girl. Now as a friend, you cannot support my decision. You do not want me so why does that matter? I love you like I love Tashay, Amar. This is not fair, and you know it. Do you think I do not know about Jermaine and Charles in my bed.? Well, guess what, I heard y'all too. That should have been me. You are the reason that I went back to Laia. Amar, you kept rejecting me over and over. Now you are telling me not to go. But the jokes on you this time because I am going whether you like it or not!" yelled Dante. He was heading out the door when Amar grabbed his arm real tight. He knocked her down to get away. Amar called out to him, but Dante did not hear her.

"Dante, please come back. I love you, too!" cried Amarylis Scott. She sat her back up against the wall and started talking to herself like she did when she was a kid. All these negative voices in her head were controlling her mind. "Amarylis you are a dirty little whore. Nobody wants you. You are so ugly and stupid. Just kill yourself. Your worthless. Your mama don't love. You are were the reason that your Grandmother killed herself "said the voices. "Stop it. Stop it please! Just leave me be! I do not want to die. I do

Sparkle Riley

not want to kill myself. Leave me alone! Just go away!"

yelled Amar.

Amarylis just laid her head in her lap. She had visions

of Birdie leaving her on the front porch. She saw and heard

Grandma Estelle splashing water in the bathtub. She saw her

wedding day as clear as day. All the guest's faces were gone,

and the church was burning in flames. It was a nightmare

while she was awake. Amar knew that she was living a life of

sin. Premarital sex,

Lying, cheating and stealing was all she knew. She needed

help bad. But who would want to help her? Amarylis was on

her knees crying when someone walked in on her.

"Amarylis, what is wrong with you girl? Get up off my

floor! Did you escape from a Psychiatric Facility in South

Carolina? I am calling the police!" screamed Siarra Jones.

"No, please Ms. Jones! Put the phone down and let me

explain. I do have issues but the crazy ones. I had a rough

day! Ms. Jones, I am an unbelievably bad person. You have

Sparkle Riley

no idea about my life at all. I just fell off the deep end again, I keep having these bizarre nightmares. At first, I had them at night while I sleep. But now I am being triggered during the day by them. I need help, Ms. Siarra! Can you please help me? I really want to be a better person. I had a fight with Dante and everything. He is leaving me like all the others. He promised to look out for me!" cried Amar.

As much as she disliked the girl, she still had a soft spot for her. It probably was because she lost Tashay. It was something touching about Amarylis. She was such a troubled young lady and she felt sorry for her. Amarylis did not have any family or friends. So, Siarra had no other choice but to help her. Somebody had to do it for the poor child so it might as well be her. Even Dante had her back and she knew why now.

"Ok, I got you. But you need to be totally honest with me Amarylis. I will help you the best way that I can. We may even need to consult with a Doctor about your anxiety and depression. It does not have to be a Psychiatrist, but at least a Therapist or Counselor. You are going to have to take accountability for some if not, all your actions. I cannot perform a miracle all by myself. You have to want to help yourself first. It is not going to be easy Amarylis. There will be bumps along the road. But I have faith in you. You can overcome these obstacles young lady. God has brought you this far, hasn't he? Let me make a quick run to Giants Dear. You need some herbs in your life. Lock the door, I will be right back, kay" said Siarra. She quickly dashed out the front door. Two seconds later, she came back in. Amar was still sitting in the same spot on the floor.

"Girl, what am I going to do with you, huh? You still have not got off my floor yet. I just came back in to switch purses. This brown one on my shoulders is a little light on cash, lol. I know that I got at least a hundred dollars in the one in my room. Do not mind me Amarylis. I have issues too" said Siarra with a smile and out she went.

Amarylis really felt like crap now. She stole money from Siarra's purse earlier. Now she was going to be real embarrassed at the Super Market! Imagine when she reaches into her wallet and her money is not there, see that is why I am going to hell! I am such a cold and ruthless person. I just enjoy being bad. It is my addiction. I can not control my actions. I don't care what Ms. Siarra says!" said Amar. She was drifting off into a daze again when she heard a knock on the door. She figured that Ms. Siarra must have forgotten something again. But it was odd that she did not use her key. So, with thinking twice about it, she opened the door. "Ms. Siarra, why did you forget now?" said Amar.

"Well, well well! If it is not Miss. Southern Peach? Are you all alone? Is Siarra or Dante here with you?" said Ricky while licking his lips. Amar knew that he was a dog on the first day she saw him. She knew his type too well. He was a smooth talker and Mack Daddy. He was using Ms. Siarra to death. Ricky had a whole bunch of women in

Sparkle Riley

Baltimore City. The fact that he was standing there lusting after her, proved her point.

"Mr. Ricky, you shouldn't be here when Ms. Siarra isn't home. I will tell her to call you when she gets home" said Amar as she tried to close the front door. But Ricky put his foot in the doorway so that she could not close it.

"Hey, that's not Southern Hospitality. I wonder what Siarra would think about your rude behavior towards me. Just let me in. I only want to talk to you. Can I get anything for you? I know that you do not have a job. Maybe I can loan you some money or something. Amarylis, we all want to help you. I am Siarra's main man. If I help you, I will score big points with her. So, let us make this a win for the both of us, you feel me?" said that low-down Ricky. Amar had to think long and hard about that one. She was in a bind and felt bad about stealing Ms. Siarra's money. She did not want to betray her. You never run game on the hand that feeds you, thought Amar.

Sparkle Riley

"Ok, you got me Sir. You can only come in for a minute because I do not want her getting the wrong idea about me. I would not want to do her dirty like that. I just need a couple of dollars Mr. Ricky. I borrowed some cash and I want to pay her back. If you lend me the money Sir, I promise to pay back every cent of it" said Amar. Ricky was aware of Amar's fragile and vulnerable state of mind. Ricky clearly had the upper hand in her situation and was going to make it his business to take advantage of the disadvantaged. He came in and closed the door behind him.

Siarra was at the cash register cussing out the cashier about her money. She kept telling the cashier that she had the money in her purse somewhere. Meanwhile, the customers in the line were becoming annoyed and agitated. A manager was called over to intervene. When it was causing a loud ruckus, security was called. Luckily for Siarra, her next- door neighbor was in Giants at the same time. Old Ms. Harris was to the rescue! Ms. Harris was a nosey old owl who watched

Sparkle Riley

the neighborhood like a Hawk. She went out of her way to lend Siarra the cash. She practically knocked customers over to get close to her. Once they reached the parking lot, Ms. Harris spoke her piece.

"Say Siarra, that prostitute in your house is giving our neighborhood a bad name. I see different men's jumping in and out of your window in the wee hours. I tell you one thing! I would not bring my man around that little Hussy. Just be careful Siarra. That girl is wicked. Watch out for Dante too" said Ms. Harris and she drove off. Siarra was speechless, she was not expecting for her to say that. Siarra got in her car and rolled down the windows. She needed some fresh air to clear her mind.

As Siarra parked outside her house, she noticed that all her lights were off. The house was pitch dark. Even Ms. Harris had her lights off too. She just figured that Amar was asleep. She did have a major meltdown earlier. Once inside, she quickly put her groceries away. She was thinking about calling Dante, but figured it was a little late. So, she called the next best thing, her man. Ricky answered on the first ring.

"Hey Bae, did I wake you? I went out to the Grocery Store. How was your day baby?" said Siarra. She missed seeing her man or talking to him. But she was not ready for the trash coming out of his mouth.

"Siarra, that girl in your house is a whore. I came by to check on you baby and I had to fight her off me. I cannot be with a woman that has a young tramp in her house. It is either me or her because one of us gots to go. I ain't trying to catch no charge. You got a good brother over here, so you better know what time it is! You need to put that bitch out, you feel me. I bet that's why Dante left! Siarra, you still with me? I do not hear no agreeing words coming out of your mouth. Bae, Bae, what's up Shorty?" said Ricky.

Siarra did not know what to do now. She had to chose between her man and her charity case. Amar was not even a part of her family for one. Between her man and Ms. Harris,

Sparkle Riley

that decision was unanimous. Amar was a bit too much to handle. Her neighbors would be raising a riot over her. Amar had an unhealthy obsession with her Son, Dante. She had mommy issues. She suffered from traumatic and unhealed experiences. Tomorrow, she was out. Siarra was willing to help her find a woman's shelter because a good man was hard to find.

CHAPTER 9

Amar woke up feeling like crap. She had a migraine headache and everything. Amar yawned and took a nice deep stretch. Amar stepped out of the bed and looked around the room. Her feet wiggled on the floor. "Hmm, that's strange. Where are my slippers? Hey, who took my robe?" yelled Amar. She got up frantically to find that her things were gone. The closets were empty. Hey now, thought Amar and that's when Ms. Siarra stood in her doorway. She stood there with a mad face and her arms folded.

"Ms. Siarra, what is going on here? All my things are gone. I do not even see my bags. Where are they and what did you do with them?" said Amar. Ms. Siarra gave her a look to kill. Amar knew what time it was.

"If this is about Mr. Ricky, I can explain. He..." said Amar but could not finish her sentence. It was obvious that her no good boyfriend got to her first.

"Save it Amarylis. I took the liberty of packing your bags. I am putting your trifling behind out. Your Uber is on its way. The driver has been paid and instructed to take you to the woman's shelter. You stole money out of my purse Amarylis. You forced my man to have sex with you! My neighbors know that you are a prostitute! You can sit your black ass on the porch to wait for the ride. You have exactly four seconds to vacate my premises!" said Ms. Siarra.

"Ms. Siarra, you are going overboard now. I will admit that I did steal your money. I was planning on paying you back for that. But I did not consent to having sex with Mr.

Sparkle Riley

Ricky. So, he grabbed me by the neck and forced me to perform sexual acts on him. You should be getting rid of him instead of me. I had to fight your boyfriend off me. I beat his behind good. He has a black eye and a busted lip. Even with all that, he still regained control of the situation. He is lying to you Ms. Siarra. Money is a materialistic thing that you can always get back. But attempted rape will stay with me forever. I can not get back those horrific moments. You have every right to hate me for stealing. I even get that you may never forgive me for that. But to side with a cheating rapist is dead wrong. He chose to attack me on his own. If he is as good as you think he is, would he do that? He had the option of loaning me the money. But he decided to take advantage of me instead! So, I will ask you again, Ms. Siarra. Do you want me to leave your home?" said Amar.

"Your four seconds is up. Be a lady and walk Amarylis. And leave my son alone, too. If I catch you around either of us, I will file for a restraining order. Amar, you need

Sparkle Riley

to get some help. Another woman would have killed you. As for me, you are not worth catching a charge for. Sooner or later you will get killed or kill yourself like your Granny did!" said Siarra.

That last comment got Siarra a punch to the face. Siarra retaliated by grabbing Amar's neck with her bare hands. A violent fight erupted into bleed shed. Glass shattered all over the rug. The ladies were trying to beat each other to death. Amar struggled to be released from Siarra's grip. Once she wiggled free of her, she ran for the door. Siarra chased behind her and the fight continued into the hallway. Seconds later, you could hear one of the ladies rolling down the flight of stairs.

Footsteps could be heard running down the steps. As Siarra stood over her, Amar reached up and grabbed her leg. Siarra's bruised body had plunged off the step. The ladies tried to rip each other's eyes out. They were biting, scratching and spitting too. Mr. Ricky came in unexpectantly.

Sparkle Riley

He liked to see two women fighting over him. It gave him a rush and a boost of confidence! First thing he did was pull out his phone to go on Facebook live. He videotaped them for a good ten-minutes before he broke up their fight. He just helped Siarra up, without saying a word. Amar crawled up from the floor in excruciating pain, as she wobbled out of the front door. Once outside, she through her bags over her shoulders and made a desperate call for help. Fifteen minutes later, Dante arrived. Amar was surprised to see him driving the other car. Where was Laia? Amar barely had enough strength to walk to the car. Dante spoke first.

"Looks like, I will be carrying my bags over my shoulders with you. Amar you called me at the right time. Come on and get in. I will explain everything to you. I guess I will always be your Knight and Shining Armor. It's about time that I trade your bags into a small diamond purse, right?" said Dante. Amar got in but was confused as hell. She had no idea what was going on? She explained everything to

Sparkle Riley

him in detail and he still came to her rescue. Amar did not know if she should rip his head off or kiss him.

"Dante, you and I are still not a couple, kay! I do not care how much you beg me to change my mind. It ain't happening and you know that already. Why are you smiling fool? Said Amar.

"Laia went to New York without me. We broke up because of you. I cannot see myself without you. I know you and my moms had a major fallout. But I have fallen in love with you and nothing can change that. I will just have to pray about it and put it all in God's hands now. As my girl, I hope you and my moms can reconcile your differences for me. I know that it will not happen overnight, but I am willing to wait patiently. Now let us start over Amar. Can you please get out of the car with your bags, please? I want to take those bags off your shoulders and open the door for you, my queen. That is with your permission of course!" said Dante. Amar did as she was told. Dante kept his word. He took her heavy

Sparkle Riley

bags off her shoulders. He kissed her bloody cheek as he opened the passenger door. Amarylis Scott got in and the rest was history. Amarylis Scott finally found her Prince Charming!

CHAPTER 10

A year later, they were celebrating their one- year anniversary together. Amar gave Dante his gift first. He was so happy with his Amar. Dante was on cloud nine. Even his mama was starting to come around. Her and Mr. Ricky broke up a few days after the fight. Amar had forgiven her a long time ago.

"Bae, remember that day that I went through your things. I never told you, but I was moved by your journal! I read every single word. You wrote such a compelling story about your sister's life. It is true that you have a heart of gold Sweetie. You would take the shirt off your back to help someone in need. I believe that Tashay's life story could help other girls like her. So, I did something, please do not get mad! Try to have an open mind, kay" said Amar.

"I will because I did something for you too. As my girl and soon to be wife, I would move mountains for you Amar. I want you to have an open mind too. But you go first Princess, lay it on me" said Dante.

Wow, if someone would have told her this a year ago, she would have beat them up. Here she is engaged and expecting her first child with the man of her dreams. Who would have thought that a country girl from South Carolina would find true love in the big city? Not, Amarylis Faye Scott! She could not hold it in any longer. So, she blurted it out!

"Dante, I submitted your journal to an agent. Someone big wants to buy your story and turn it into a television movie. You are going to be super rich and you will be honoring your sister's legacy. With the money you can set up a drug addiction clinic for troubled youth. The sky is the limit with your talents. I love you so much Dante Alston!" cried Amar.

"Wow, I am speechless Amar! We will be rich together from the bottom up. I want you by my side to build Tashay's legacy. You are making me cry a river over here Girlie. I hope you will be just as happy with my gift to you, too. Speaking of the past, I did a little digging and snooping too. I want our baby to be a part of both of our families. Amar, I found Birdie Scott and she lives right here in Woodlawn. I know that you probably have a grudge toward her Princess. But life is too short. You only get one mother. Yes, Birdie did wrong and she has made a few mistakes. But at the end of the day, she is still your mother. I hope one day that you can forgive her like I have. Birdie had a good reason why she left you like that. It is not my place to tell you about it. Your mama has to Princess. Even if you never want to speak to her again, at least hear her out, kay. You need this closure Honey. I hope that we all can come together as a family one day. I have her phone number and address to give to you whenever you are ready. There's no pressure, you must do what your heart tells you Amar" cried Dante.

"You are right, I am not ready to walk down that road right now. I cannot promise you that I ever will be. I need to work on me first. I want to be a good wife and mother to our child. Once I am in a good place, I will see. It is too hard for me to revisit my past now. I have to lookout for the safety of our baby right now. I want our lives to be picture perfect. I want to have a better relationship with God and your mother, Dante" cried Amar.

"I understand, no worries or pressure for you and our baby. I have a feeling though that everything is going to be alright. I know that you did not come all the way up here by coincidence. It was our fate and destiny Amar. If, I am breathing, you will never have to carry another bag over your

Sparkle Riley

shoulder. I vow to protect, respect and keep you safe like the

air I breathe, Mrs. Amarylis Jones" said her future husband.

The end

Sparkle Riley

www.ingramcontent.com/pod-product-compliance
Lightning Source LLC
Chambersburg PA
CBHW071953150726
47999CB00001B/430